BREAKING
BOUNDARIES

BREAKING *BOUNDARIES*

A FOURPLAY NOVEL

GEMMA BLYTHE

If you'd like to know if this book contains any elements that might be of concern for you, please check out the following webpage for details:

https://www.gemmablythe.com/content-notes

To Jess, Livy, and Sarah, whose consistent cheerleading and willingness
to take 'one last glance' made this book possible.

Chapter One

"PADIDDLE!" MY BEST FRIEND Darcy yells, slamming her hand on the car ceiling. A moment later her husband's hand is on the ceiling as well, though thankfully, he's kept his right one on the steering wheel.

I look at my own husband, who's sitting next to me in the back seat, and shrug. I don't know what padiddle means, nor do I know why we're touching the ceiling.

Rafe shrugs back, though he makes the wise move of reaching upwards. "Padiddle, I guess?"

"Strip, Bex!" Darcy calls, a little too gleefully, and I just stare at her blankly.

"Say what?"

"Is padiddle not a Texas thing?" Alec asks, the only one of us who grew up out of state. "Whenever you see a car without a headlight or taillight, touch the ceiling and yell it. Last one takes an item of clothing off."

"No, it's not," I say. "Or at least, it's not a *me* thing. I should get a pass since I didn't know the rules."

"Nope," Darcy says. "Take it off."

I'm wearing shorts and a tank top—there's not a lot of clothes to spare. "Take what off? I'm not exactly—"

She interrupts me, clapping as she shouts, "Take it off! Take it off!"

Alec joins in next, hitting his hand against the steering wheel. "Take it off! Take it off!"

And then my husband betrays me, giving another shrug before adding to the chant.

"You," I say, squinting my eyes at him and then slicing my finger across my neck. Rafe just winks one gorgeous brown eye at me.

But it's our first kid-free vacation in I don't know how long, and who knows the next time we'll get grandparents babysitting at the same time as our best friends. Plus, I'm wearing flip flops and have decided shoes count, so I play along.

"Fine." I present a hot pink flip-flop with a flourish.

"Yaaaay!" Everyone gives me appropriate applause, and I mock-bow, then check my phone. Four and a half more hours until we reach our Airbnb in South Padre. How many padiddles could we really come across?

***

I'm not wearing pants by the time we arrive. Alec only lost once, and he took his shirt off because it was the easiest thing to do while driving. Darcy is down to her underwear—she lost twice and had kicked her flip flops off as soon as we got in the car, so Alec insisted she couldn't count them. And Rafe, somehow, is fully dressed.

"It's because you're the tallest so you started off closest to the ceiling," I say grumpily when we get out. He grins and kisses me, then gives my ass a gentle slap.

I laugh and shove him playfully, then turn to Alec who is pulling suitcases out of the trunk.

"Babe, we're only here for a week, how much did you pack?" he asks Darcy, who shrugs and tugs on the suitcase, seemingly unbothered by the fact that she's only wearing panties and a bra.

Though, to be fair, it's a super cute set that flatters her figure. "Where'd you get them?" I ask, motioning, and she grins.

"Panache! I'm a little obsessed with their stuff." She cups a hand around her mouth and stage-whispers, "Alec is too."

I laugh and glance at Alec, who raises his hands guiltily and tosses Darcy a wink. I'm sure the guys know that we talk about our sex lives—and have for *years*. After all, it was in our dorm room freshman year of college that she lost her virginity (to be clear, I wasn't there, though she gave me all the fun details later.) And she was the first person I told when Rafe and I slept together senior year ("I think he's The One," I told her, and it turns out I was right.) Now that we're in our thirties the discussions are different than they were back then—feeling self-conscious about the post-baby body, how to balance a sex life with three children, that sort of thing—but occasionally there'll be something fun and sexy to tell, and Darcy is always the first person I go to.

Alec reaches over and wraps an arm around Darcy, pulling her in for a kiss, and I watch for a moment before looking away to give them privacy. They're a gorgeous couple—I wish I wore my curves with the kind of confidence Darcy has, and while I'm obsessed with my husband there's no denying the fact that Alec is the hottest guy I know in real life. So you can't blame me for taking a beat before turning to Rafe, who wraps his arm around my waist and rests a hand on my ass to give it a squeeze.

"I think if we don't stop them, they'll start humping against the car," he whispers in my ear and I laugh, pulling away and threading our fingers together.

I tug him towards the door of the Airbnb while pulling up the instructions on how to get in.

"Doubtful." I glance back to see Alec whispering something against Darcy's hair. She laughs, giving him a playful shove, and I add, "It's not that kind of trip."

Chapter Two

THE RENTAL IS A cute little house. It has two bedrooms with king-sized beds, a living room with a large open space in front of the TV, and a gorgeous kitchen. Outside there's a hot tub, but no pool, probably because it's just a couple of blocks from the beach.

I'm unpacking the groceries we brought when Darcy and Alec finally make it inside. She's pulled her shirt on, but he hasn't, toned chest on full display.

I do my best not to stare even though there are few things on a guy I love more than the V-shaped cut of an Adonis belt.

Then Rafe's arms are around me and he's behind me, whispering in my ear.

"You can look all you want, but I'm still your favorite, right?"

I flush because I've been caught, but laugh and turn around, wrapping my arms around his neck. His torso may not be as defined as Alec's, but it's still one of my favorite things to stare at, to trace, to draw patterns on with fingers and then lips and then tongue until he's begging for me to go a little further south.

"Of course," I say. "I wouldn't trade you for a dozen Alecs."

"Hmmmm, a dozen?" Rafe grins. "I'm not entirely sure I can say the same."

An image of the two of them together flashes in my mind and I can't help but find it a little intriguing. "I'll allow it if you promise to let me watch," I say, joking.

Mostly.

He laughs against my mouth as he slips his tongue past my lips, and I let him in eagerly. It tangles with mine as he pins my hips to the counter behind me and his hand slips just past the hem of my shirt, resting against my back.

His thumb strokes my skin there softly, and I want more. I consider making a flimsy excuse and dragging him to the room we claimed. Having three kids—the youngest of which crawls into bed with us around midnight at least half the time—means our sex life isn't quite what either of us would consider ideal. It's a pattern of famine and feast—some weeks we have it every day, other times we go days or even weeks without.

Needless to say, I'm very much counting on this being a feast week.

Darcy's voice rings out from the closest bedroom. "No fair, you guys claimed the bigger room!"

Rafe pulls his head away from mine, though he keeps the rest of our bodies flush against each other. Through his shorts I can feel him thickening against my stomach.

"The rooms are the same size, but we did pick the one with the better bathroom," he calls to her.

"Oh my God this bathtub," she yells a moment later, and I laugh. "And how many shower heads are in this walk-in?"

"Three for each of us," I call, grinning at Rafe.

"Holy shit, there are twelve?" Alec asks.

"No, you weirdo, six! You're not invited into our shower."

Alec's head pops into the kitchen, and he grins. "Can't blame a guy for trying."

Darcy shows up behind him, mouth in a pout. "We should put our stuff in the room with the crap bathroom, Alec."

"You'll survive," I promise her, and not even the puppy-dog eyes she tosses my way will make me give up the room we claimed. I've been dreaming of that bathtub since I saw the listing online.

"Once everyone is settled in, we can head to the beach?" Rafe suggests, and that brings back a smile to Darcy's face as she bounds back to her room.

An hour later we're on the beach, Darcy and I stretched out on towels while the guys kick a soccer ball around. Rafe played throughout high school and college, and now he plays with Alec in a rec league every fall.

"Is it really that much better than an IUD?" Darcy asks, squinting in my direction, and I shrug.

"I was always paranoid with the IUD, and the vasectomy makes me way less anxious. But if you're happy with yours, I'm sure it's basically the same."

"Rafael should talk to him about it. Alec is such a wimp sometimes."

I grin. "So should I tell Rafe that you told me to tell him to talk to Alec about getting the snip?"

Darcy laughs. "Okay, okay. Maybe I'll just bring it up at dinner. 'Hey Rafael, Bex told me your sex life improved, like, tenfold once you got a vasectomy. Do you agree?'"

"That'll go over great," I joke, watching him kick the ball to Alec and thinking about the quickie we had before heading over. He'd caught me when I was about to pull on my swimsuit bottoms, spinning me around and bending me over the bed.

"At the beach we're both going to know I came inside you right before we left." His mouth was right by my ear as he fucked me from behind, fingers working my clit. "I'm gonna fill you, then pull these up"—he crumpled my bottoms against the bed—"and it'll be our little secret."

Then a vibration against my clit made me gasp softly against the comforter. We brought a couple of toys with us and he'd grabbed one of the smaller vibes, biting my earlobe as he held me still with his free hand.

"We don't have much time, so you get to come quickly. But tonight I'm going to make up for it. I'm going to fuck you so slowly, and bring you to the edge and back at least a dozen times. I want to hear you whimper and beg for my cock, want you to promise to do whatever I ask. Maybe I'll have you suck me off, would you like that?"

The answer to that is obvious, of course. I love his cock, love going down on him, love when he fists my hair and groans and begs. He likes to pretend fucking my mouth is a power move for him, but we both know that I love it just as much. Half the time I'm humping my own fingers at the same time, so turned on that I'm impatient for my turn. Getting off while Rafe's dick is in my mouth is one of my favorite things ever.

He ticked up the vibration a notch while his teeth nipped at my shoulder and the hand that had been holding me still slipped between me and the comforter, under my bikini top to tweak a nipple. The coil of my body started to tighten and I pulled a knee up on the bed so I could thrust back against him.

"I'm gonna," I gasped quietly, and felt him nod behind me.

"Fuck yeah, you are," he growled in my ear. "You're gonna come all over my cock and then I'm gonna come and you'll carry me around all fucking day. Come for me Rebecca, do it."

Another squeeze of my tit and I was gone, thrown over the edge, my body clenching around him, squeezing his cock. And he came too, shoving himself deep inside me.

"Rafe," I whimpered because he hadn't let up the vibrator. He chuckled against my ear, knowing he was walking me along the edge of pleasure and torture. And then, just when it was about to be too much, he pulled it away, collapsing against me and pinning me to the bed.

Back on the beach, he grins at me and wiggles his eyebrows. I suspect we're both remembering our encounter and the fact that I'm still filled with him. That when he slides his fingers in me later, he'll be able to feel the evidence of this afternoon's encounter.

"Earth to Bex!"

It's Darcy, and when I turn to look at her, she's grinning. "Thinking about Rafael's dick?"

I laugh and turn over, laying on my stomach so she can't see my nipples harden and poke through my suit. "I plead the fifth," I say, which basically confirms that yes, I was.

"Not that I blame you. Getting alone time with our men is pretty much the whole point of this trip, right?"

I laugh and then stick out my bottom lip in a pout. "I thought the point was spending time with your best friend."

She grins and lays back, stretching her long tan legs out, and throws one of her arms over her eyes to block the sun. "I guess we can do that too."

And really, great sex with Rafe, time with best friends, a childfree week, and this gorgeous weather? I'm pretty sure it doesn't get much better than this.

Chapter Three

"DID YOU GUYS BREAK in the shower?" Darcy asks as we eat dinner that night. Rafe and I don't answer, but the look we exchange across the table probably answers it for us.

"Ugh," she groans dramatically. "I'm so jealous. There's barely enough room to bend over in ours."

Technically we didn't do any bending over, just watching. I stood against one wall and made good use of one of the shower heads, while Rafe watched me and stroked himself. Is there anything hotter than watching a guy get off, knowing you're what he's fantasizing about? Even after years of marriage, over a decade of being with the same guy, I love the way it makes me feel desirable and wanted.

Plus, Rafe is hot as fuck, so it's not like watching him play with his cock is a chore.

"You'll live, I promise," I say, and Darcy rolls her eyes but grins.

"So Rafael, Bex says you're up for a promotion?" she asks, and the conversation changes to more benign topics: who's going to take over as PTA president next year after Darcy's term, and how our boys are almost old enough for middle school.

We each have three kids, pretty close in age. Our oldest—both boys—are in fifth grade. Rafe and I have a daughter in third and a son in first, they've got a daughter in fourth and a son in second. The kids have grown up together for the most part—Darcy and Alec were living in Charlotte when their oldest was born but moved to Texas when she was pregnant with her second. And even though Rafe and Alec aren't as close as Darcy and I are—who could be, really—they get along well.

The summer before our freshman year, chance (via a faceless university housing administrator) set the gears turning on this friendship that not only lasted, but grew. And after dinner, when we're stretched out in the living room watching a movie—Darcy's feet in Alec's lap, Rafe's head in mine—I'm thankful for it. Not just for the four of us, but for our kids, who will have friends that have known them their whole life, who they'll have shared memories with—everything from backyard barbecues to Disney trips. It's special, the sort of thing they'll remember when they're older and hopefully try to emulate with their own friends. I don't know what I'd be without this support system.

"What're you thinking?" Darcy asks. "You're staring at Alec rubbing my feet."

I laugh self-consciously, running my fingers through Rafe's hair. "Just that I'm glad we've got you guys as friends."

Darcy's face softens and she smiles. "The feeling is mutual. Love you," she says, then her grin turns cheeky. "Even though you stole the better shower."

I burst out laughing, reach for a pillow, and hurl it across the room. "Give it up already."

Rafe pipes up from my lap. "If you behave, maybe we'll let you use it one day."

"Yeah?" Darcy asks.

"I don't know about that," I say to Rafe. "She'll pester us every day asking if she's earned it."

He wags his finger at Darcy playfully. "True. In that case, part of behaving is not pestering us daily."

"Now she's going to pester *me* daily," Alec says dramatically. "Asking if I think she did a good job."

"I'm not a toddler!" Darcy says, then stands up, playing at being haughty and tugs Alec's hand. "I can tell where I'm not wanted. We're going to bed!"

She winks, though, to let us know she's joking.

Alec stands up, tipping an imaginary cap. "Goodnight, I guess."

"Night!" Rafe and I call back.

I blow Darcy a kiss. She bats it away, flipping me off, and then the door to their bedroom shuts securely behind them.

***

An hour later when we go to our room, we can hear them. At first, it's subtle, some groans and quiet mutterings from Alec. Rafe strips down to his boxers and I pull on his discarded shirt and we politely pretend to not know what's going on.

By the time we're done brushing our teeth and are crawling into bed, Alec has gone quiet.

But she's the one making noises.

Rafe and I glance at each other, then laugh quietly. "There were a few reviews about noise traveling, but I assumed they meant, like, the living room. Not that the bedroom walls were paper thin," I whisper.

"Their bed is right up against the same wall," he says, gesturing. "So they're, like, right there."

We look at the wall behind our headboard, knowing theirs is just on the other side. I get a mental image that I probably shouldn't—Darcy on her knees for Alec while he fucks her mouth. That's probably why we couldn't hear her when we came in, because she was occupied with his dick, muffling any noises she was making.

But now I'm pretty sure he's going down on her, because the wall is thin enough that I can hear the occasional word. *Fuck* and *there* and *yes* and *baby* and *Alec* and *more* and *don't stop.*

"She's pretty loud," I whisper to Rafe, and he grins at me in the dark.

"Some people are pretty loud."

"But usually it sounds like they're faking it. This definitely sounds real."

My orgasms tend to be quiet. I gasp against Rafe's skin, moan into his mouth, speak in hushed tones. I know this because we taped ourselves once. It was our anniversary and we were a little drunk, a little high, and taking full advantage of a child-free night. After watching porn we decided to try and make some ourselves. It was hot, but the next morning I insisted on deleting it. Sometimes I think of trying it again, to see how we sound and look on different occasions, but I'm always concerned that the risk isn't really worth the payoff.

But unlike me in our homemade video, Darcy is loud. And like I told Rafe, it sounds real. It doesn't sound like a movie, where it's obvious they're acting.

I wonder what a tape of Darcy and Alec would be like.

Rafe's voice cuts through my thoughts. "You like it?"

I look over at him, he's smirking. I roll my eyes.

"Well, yeah, they're hot. You don't?"

He snakes his hand into my underwear, finds me wet, and his grin widens.

"No, you *really* like it."

There's a pause in the sounds coming through the wall, and I think they're done. I almost *hope* they're done, because I shouldn't be getting this turned on by them. For the sake of our friendship it would be best if there's only silence from that side of the wall for the rest of the week.

But then they start up again, and I can hear both of them. He's done going down on her and now they're fucking.

My pussy clenches at that realization and Rafe's finger is still probing me gently so he feels it.

He chuckles.

"Shut up," I say, burying my face in his chest so he can't see me blush. Apparently I'm a teenager again, blushing when it comes to sex stuff. "It's hot, okay?"

"It is," he says, finding my clit with his fingers and applying the perfect amount of pressure. He knows me so well and can unlock me like no one else has ever been able to. I sigh against his skin.

"I'm also really digging that you find it hot. Tell me what you think they're doing."

"Rafe," I say, looking up at him, because he's talking about our best friends here. "We have to sit across from them at the table tomorrow morning."

"Is he on top or is she?"

"He is," I say immediately, without thinking. That's what I'm picturing—she's spread out under him, feet flat on the bed as she arches up towards him. He's propped up on his elbows, muscles straining as he holds himself off her so that he can nip at her tits. This time the 'V' of his Adonis belt doesn't disappear under his shorts. It points exactly where it's meant to: right at the cock that's fucking her, that's disappearing and reappearing with every thrust. Maybe every once in a while, they glance down and watch themselves, watch as his cock slides in and out of her pussy, thick and fast and hard.

From the other side of the wall, I can tell their pace based on her moans, and the way they're punctuated every second or so.

"Tell me more," Rafe says, and I can't believe we're doing this, but I do it anyway. I tell him everything I'm picturing, how she slaps his ass and scratches at his back. How she grasps his hair to pull him away from one tit and direct him to the other, and how that long, low moan she just made could be because he scraped her nipple with his teeth.

Rafe starts thrusting his fingers into me in time with the rhythm we're hearing, and I wrap my hand around his cock. It's like we're doing this all together, all four of us, except they don't know we're participating. But when he starts to groan I press my mouth against his, capturing his noise.

"We can't let them hear," I whisper. "They'll be so embarrassed."

I'm not entirely sure that's true—Darcy's more open when it comes to sex than I am. If they heard us, I'd probably die of embarrassment. But if tomorrow we told them that we could hear they'd just shrug it off. Laugh and apologize and say that they hope we got a good show.

Still, I don't think I want them to know that we heard. I'm afraid they'd be able to tell just how much I enjoyed it.

He nods and rests his forehead against mine. We pant as we fuck each other with our hands. "Shit," I whisper when he brushes his thumb against my clit.

"Fuck," he groans quietly when I reach for his balls with my free hand.

"I'm gonna," he says eventually, and I shake my head, slowing down my hand.

"Hold on, I'm not quite..."

But then he strokes my G-spot. Rafe isn't the only guy I've slept with, but he's the only one that's ever figured out that part of me. He's the one who discovered that with the right touch I can come in no time at all. We've started jokingly calling it my instant orgasm button.

The catch is, it's the one thing I'm not quiet about.

"Fuck," I groan, and it's loud. Louder than any other noise we've made, and for a moment there's silence on the other side of the wall. Shit. Did they hear us? We freeze, my hand wrapped around Rafe's cock and his fingers buried deep in my pussy, barely even breathing, until we hear some whispers—I can't make out the words—and the noises start up again.

I tell myself this is good, but only because I'd have felt bad if we'd killed their groove.

Rafe's fingers graze my G-spot again and I shake my head, not sure I can be as quiet as we need to be. His grin is wicked as he holds up a clean finger to his mouth, signaling that he wants me to try, and then rubs his thumb across my clit.

I bury my face in his neck, sucking on the skin there, hard, to keep my mouth busy and quiet. His fingers keep moving, focusing mostly on my clit, but occasionally he brushes against my G-spot, and I know it's on purpose. He's teasing me and even though it makes staying quiet harder, and I fucking love it.

My hand speeds up again, and soon we're both moving at the same tempo, matching the rhythm of the noises from the other side of the wall. I swear they're louder now, they're not even attempting to be quiet, almost like they know we're listening and getting off on it, even though that's ridiculous.

It's obviously not the case.

"Bex," Rafe gasps, and I can tell by the way he's losing control that he's close, and he focuses on my G-spot to make sure I'm as close as him. I whimper against his skin, trying to be quiet, to not reveal ourselves to Darcy and Alec. I dig the nails of my free hand into Rafe's back to try and hold on, knowing my frantic suckling at his neck is leaving a hickey that's going to be impossible to hide.

And then I gasp and come, body spasming in time with every stroke of Rafe's fingers. A millisecond later I feel Rafe's warm release on my stomach, and then almost immediately I hear Darcy on the other side of the wall.

She's so fucking loud as she comes. Dramatic, which fits with her personality. Yelling Alec's name, swearing, moaning, and then there's a groan that's unmistakably Alec. Honestly, hearing the two of them orgasm at almost the exact same time we did, just a few feet away—even though we're separated by a wall—stirs something deep in me that I can't fully put into words. I look at Rafe and he looks the same, like he's a little bewildered and doesn't want to pick at why, because these are our best friends and we probably shouldn't have done this.

"They can never know," I whisper, still out of breath from the orgasm and what we just did. He nods.

"We probably shouldn't have..." he starts, then stops and looks embarrassed, as if he's not sure he should finish the sentence.

I chew on my bottom lip for a second before adding, "It was really fucking hot, though."

A look of relief crosses his face, like he's glad to discover that we both apparently have this same kink. He pulls off my shirt to wipe us off, and then I go to the bathroom to clean up. When I come back out, he motions me to the bed. And when I crawl in he flips me on my back and hovers over me for a kiss.

It's a soft one, gentle. We've used up all our sexual energy for the night, but this is intimacy, romance, love.

He confirms it by following up with a quiet, "I love you."

"Love you too," I say, and he gives me one more kiss before stripping my underwear off. He pulls my back to his chest and slips his arm between my breasts as we spoon. We're both naked, skin to skin all the way down, and I snuggle against him, comfortable, safe, and loved.

Chapter Four

The next morning I take my time getting ready, not wanting to face Darcy and Alec.

"It's not that big a deal," Rafe insists as I pull my swimsuit on. Apparently I'm the only one whose dreams consisted of the two of us sitting in a big armchair in the corner of their room, watching as Darcy rides Alec, or as he fucks her doggie style, tits bouncing with every thrust.

Really, what's wrong with me? Fantasizing about women is nothing new, but fantasizing about Darcy? That definitely is. I don't understand why I can't get the idea of her and Alec out of my head.

Rafe can tell that I'm distracted. He drops down to my eye level. "Stop thinking about Alec's dick," he teases.

My face flushes warm, because that's not what's keeping my mind occupied. "I think I'm more interested in Darcy's boobs than Alec's dick," I confess. "I mean, I'm sure his dick is great—after all, the rest of him is. But if I had to choose..."

"Hot." He wraps his arms around me and nibbles softly at my neck, the tiny bites tickling my skin. "Can I watch?"

"Shut up." I give his shoulder a playful shove, laughing. "And no more hickeys—yours is big enough for both of us."

"It really is." He pulls away, examining the big purple bruise I left on his neck in the mirror. It's the price he paid for playing with my G-spot while I was trying to keep Darcy and Alec from hearing us. "Too bad it's not turtleneck season."

"I'm sorry," I say, shrugging irreverently.

"How about next time you leave one where they can't see?"

I give him a *look*. "Like your dick?"

"Please don't bruise my dick," he starts, then smirks. "Actually, why don't you try. No teeth, just sucking."

He gives my neck another soft nip and I push him away, laughing. "Maaaaybe," I say as I turn around with a swish of my hips. I'm entering the kitchen before I realize he's distracted me enough to leave the bedroom. When he walks in behind me, I point at him accusingly. He just wiggles his eyebrows, giving me another one of his irresistible smiles.

"Gonna let us in on the joke?" Alec asks.

Rafe doesn't look up as he pours us coffee. "Nope."

The kitchen has a little bar where Alec and Darcy are sitting, and I settle next to her. "Did you guys sleep well?" I ask.

Instead of responding, Darcy starts coughing, choking on her orange juice.

Shit. For a second there I'd forgotten about overhearing them.

Alec thumps her back a couple of times until she can speak again. Motioning to her throat, she says, "Sorry. Wrong pipe."

Rafe has started frying eggs for breakfast sandwiches, assembling them as we make small talk, and I make a sincere effort to avoid any discussion of last night.

But when Rafe turns to give Darcy her plate, she frowns. "What happened to your neck?"

"Curling iron," Rafe says smoothly, and Alec snorts, holding up his plate for the food.

"Your hair does look good, though," Alec says, and Rafe pretends to toss his hair over his shoulder.

"Hey!" I say with a laugh. "Watch yourself, I'm right here!"

Rafe shrugs. "Sorry, babe, I've got a thing for guys who play soccer."

"I mean, I can understand that. I've got a weakness for them myself." I prop my chin up on my hand and gaze at Rafe, batting my eyelashes at him playfully. Eventually he looks my way with a grin, and I fan myself, pretending to swoon.

"Speaking of giving each other hickeys," Darcy says once she's swallowed her first mouthful of food, "Have I earned the shower yet?"

"Oh my God," I say dramatically, raising my hands in mock-exasperation.

"Stop asking!" Alec says, before Rafe can chime in, and all four of us laugh.

***

Our plans for the day are obvious—you don't drive five hours to the Texas coast and not spend your first morning at the beach. Even if it *is* just a Texas beach.

"Another two-piece?" Darcy asks as I slip out of my cover-up once we've arrived.

It's a legitimate question, considering I tend to pick more modest swimsuits. But I figured this was the trip to try something new, so I only brought two pieces—real ones, not just a tankini. My stomach might not be as flat as I'd like, and my thighs might be a bit thicker than they used to be, but I'm going to rock the hell out of my suits anyway. I'm approaching forty, but we're with friends who aren't going to judge me, and based on the way Rafe watched me wriggle into my suit this morning, he's a fan.

"I'm trying to step out of my comfort zone," I admit, and Darcy grins, eyes trailing down my body and then back up again.

"It looks really good, Bex."

As she speaks my eyes get drawn to her mouth where she's licking her lips. Her tongue is the perfect shade of pink and her lips lo—

These are the exact sort of things I've never thought about her before this trip. The sort of things I shouldn't be thinking about my best friend.

"Thanks." I gesture to her suit. "You too, though."

Today she's wearing a one piece that's just as unreasonably sexy as the one she wore yesterday. Like me, Darcy's body is probably what people would consider pretty average, but when I look at her all I see is how great she looks. Yesterday's suit was eggplant-colored and strappy, with cutouts along the sides, and I've spent a not-insignificant amount of time trying to avoid thinking about the tan lines it would leave. The way she'd look naked, stretched out, a patchwork of pale and golden skin.

Today's suit is black, but to call it a deep 'V' would be an understatement. The neckline almost reaches her belly button, and I'm not entirely sure what's keeping it in place. A large wave could probably flip the fabric over her boob. When she starts playfully striking modeling poses, I smile and then scan the water for Rafe so that I have an excuse to look anywhere other than the expanse of skin in front of me.

I'm also wondering if the waves are large enough to knock Darcy's swimsuit off-kilter. I decide they probably aren't, and stand up to find my husband.

"Hey," he says a minute later, when I've excused myself and caught up to him. Instead of answering I grab his hand and drag him further into the water, only stopping when it's halfway up my chest.

He raises his eyebrows at me. "You okay?"

I nod and glance to make sure there isn't anyone near us, then reach over, grasping him lightly through his swim trunks.

"Whoa." He laughs, but his hand grips my wrist. "What's bringing this on?"

I wrinkle my nose, considering whether or not to be honest, but it's Rafe, and we talk about these things. "Feeling guilty because I'm having dirty thoughts about someone other than you."

He grins. "Alec?"

"No."

The grin widens. "Darcy?"

"Shut up and let me give you a penance hand job!"

His expression changes from teasing to serious, thumb softly stroking the underside of my wrist. "You know you don't have to get me off just because you had dirty thoughts about someone else, right? So long as I'm the one you come home to at the end of the day, you're allowed all the dirty thoughts you can handle."

What he's saying makes sense, and we're honest with each other when we find other people attractive. One of the benefits of my being bi is that a lot of the time we notice the same women—it turns out we have similar tastes. But this feels different.

"It's just weird. It's not dirty thoughts about the barista at Epoch, it's Darcy. If you were having dirty thoughts about Alec—"

"I'm not having dirty thoughts about Alec!" he interrupts, and I roll my eyes.

"I know, that's why it's called a hypothetical. *If*, babe, *if* you were. Wouldn't that be weird?"

He takes a deep breath. "Well if I were, do you think I'd need to go down on you every time? Should we start an orgasm exchange where every time we have dirty thoughts, we get each other off?"

I roll my eyes. "Obviously you wouldn't have to tell me. Nor would you owe me orgasms."

He doesn't say anything, instead just raises his eyebrows.

"Fine," I say with a mock-beleaguered sigh. "I won't give you a hand job."

His face turns back to playful and his grip around my wrist tightens as I start to pull away.

"Whoa whoa whoa. All we determined is that you don't *have* to give me a hand job. Not that you *can't*. Two totally different things here," he says.

"So, you want one?" I give his cock a quick squeeze and there's a sharp intake of breath.

"Have I ever said no?"

I fix him with a stare.

"Look, a hand job under the table at a restaurant the first time I met your parents doesn't count."

He's probably right, but I'll still hold it over him forever. I pull him down for a kiss with the hand that isn't rubbing him through his trunks. He groans, and I laugh.

"You gotta look casual, babe. Not like I'm getting you off."

Rafe takes a deep breath, and then shoots me a wink. "Can do."

I think he does a pretty good job of looking like he's *not* getting a hand job in the middle of the ocean. I know, of course, because I've cataloged what his arousal looks like: the way his breath hitches, the way his jaw flexes, the tension in his neck. He lets out the tiniest little groan and it's all I can do to keep from pushing my bottoms aside and fingering myself at the same time, but we're deep enough in the water that I need the other hand stretched out to keep the waves from tipping me over.

"You owe me."

He nods.

"You're going to get such a generous payback, mi vida," he says, "I'll peel your swimsuit off slowly, watching you shiver as the air hits your skin. Then I'll chase your suit with my lips and tongue and teeth. Tasting all the ocean salt on your skin. Covering your newly exposed skin with my mouth."

I sigh as he wiggles his eyebrows and continues, "I love the way you squirm, the way you whimper when I tweak your tits, how you spread your legs a little further open for me so that I can see your pussy all warm and wet and waiting. But I won't go there yet. First, I'll focus on your thighs. Stroking the skin there, leading up to but not going where you want me to. It'll make you open wider and beg and try to push yourself against me for release. I fucking love teasing you."

"Like you're doing now?" I ask, seriously considering letting go of him and just taking care of myself. It would serve him right.

He nods, and I feel him hold back another groan, his abs contracting as he does, showing off definition I'd trace with my tongue if we were in private.

"Don't look now," he says, which is a guaranteed way to get me to look once I know where. "But I think Darcy and Alec are doing the same thing we are."

I turn to where he's looking, ignoring his 'I told you not to', and they're about a hundred feet away, at similar depth. Darcy is looking in our direction, and I see her face get pink, but she doesn't glance away when our eyes meet.

"I see both her hands," I point out, because they're spread out, just under the surface of the water.

I can hear the grin in his voice when he replies, "Yeah, but neither of Alec's."

The thought that Alec's fingers are in her pussy right now almost takes my breath away, and my hand speeds up.

"You're thinking of her again," Rafe says, and guilt twists in my gut.

"Fuck. Yes, sorry."

"Don't be." He reaches out, running his fingers through my hair. "Especially not if I get to be there too."

And that's how the image of me with one set of fingers around Rafe's cock and the other in Darcy's pussy is planted in my mind.

I groan.

"You like that, don't you?" he asks, and I nod, sneaking a glance back at Darcy and Alec who are having a conversation of their own.

One that's completely different than ours, I'm sure, but a girl can pretend.

Rafe glances over at Alec and Darcy again and I tighten my grip, increasing my speed as I follow his stare. They're watching us too.

"Do you think they know?" I whisper, and he shrugs.

"I honestly don't give a fuck. No way to prove either way."

I kind of don't care either, especially since they're probably doing it too, but I still turn to Rafe so that it's not quite as obvious. It looks like it takes effort for him to tear his eyes away from them. We just watch each other as I speed up my hand and reach under him with my other to give his balls a little tug.

"Love you," he grunts as his breath speeds up, and I grin at him.

"Love you, too."

His abs tighten again, and I know he's on the edge. "I'm gonna," he whispers, and I nod encouragingly.

A moment later, he does.

Afterwards, I wrap my arms around his waist and rest my head against his shoulder while he pulls me into an embrace. I can feel his heart pounding in his chest, and it's always a bit of a power trip to know that I did that, that he's breathless and blissed out because of me.

"She's gonna," Rafe says, and then shifts so that I'm facing Darcy and Alec just in time to see her clap both hands over her mouth and rest her forehead on his shoulder. I'm assuming the hands are to muffle whatever sounds she's making, so in my head I play the soundtrack we heard last night, and my whole body flushes.

"Damn," I say, looking up at Rafe.

I expect him to be watching them too—he kept glancing over there while I was getting him off, after all—but he's watching me, and his eyes just set me on fire again.

"Watching you watch her is..." He stops, but I can tell by his expression that the overall sentiment is a positive one. "It makes me want to bend you over and fuck you until we're both completely spent."

"Tonight," I say with a coy little look, and he chuckles.

"Hot as last night was, I'm really starting to regret getting a place with thin walls."

I'd forgotten. Damn. I cover my face with my hands and then rest it against his chest. "Shit! Okay, bathroom sex the rest of the time we're here."

Disappointing, but doable. I'd love to get fucked on a bed sometime this week, but getting fucked by Rafe is great, no matter where.

"C'mon," I say, pulling away and tugging him towards the beach. "Let's get back before they notice how closely we're watching."

Chapter Five

We leave the beach early in the afternoon and head home for a shower and a nap. It's in the shower that Rafe decides to return the favor from earlier, using his hands and then his tongue to bring me to the edge of orgasm so many times I lose count. I finally grab his hair to hold him still, spread my legs a little further, and put my pussy against his mouth.

"Stay there until I come," I say, tightening my fingers in his hair. "No pulling away until I let go, and no more teasing."

He raises his eyebrows and I feel his mouth turn up in a grin against me, then feel his hot breath. His tongue traces my folds, then circles around my opening—wide at first then smaller and smaller, approaching but never entering. I tighten my grip, pushing him more firmly against me and he chuckles, then, *finally*, fucks me with his tongue.

With a sigh I lean against the shower wall. After a minute he replaces his tongue with a finger, then two. His tongue focuses on my clit moving up and down, then back and forth, then patterns I can't even recognize. Every gasp and moan garners a repeat of whatever movement caused it, and I get closer and closer to my peak.

"Rafe," I whimper, moving against him. "I'm close."

He redoubles his efforts, the pressure from his tongue stronger, fingers fucking me faster, and I ride his mouth until my release, my whole body shaking as I become jerkier and my thighs clench around his head.

"Fuck," I sob as my orgasm hits me, thankful that the water cascading around us will muffle my noises and keep this orgasm just for us.

He shifts from kneeling to sitting and I slide into his lap, head tucked under his chin as the water continues to stream around us. Once I've recovered, I give him a kiss, smiling as I taste myself on him.

"I love bossy Bex," he says with a grin, and I laugh.

"She makes an appearance when you take too long to get to the good stuff," I tease, and his eyes twinkle as he shakes his head.

"Making you wait *is* the good stuff, mi vida. But so is bossy Bex, so it's a win-win."

He stands up and offers a hand for me to take. After we dry off, we slip between the sheets naked for a much-needed nap. Edging always requires one.

***

Eventually we wake up and make our way out to the living room, trying to figure out a plan for the rest of the night. Not in the mood to cook, we order pizza for dinner and convince Alec to make everyone margaritas. It's rare that we all get to drink without having to worry about designated drivers or childcare, so we take advantage of it tonight, each of us having a drink more than we would under normal circumstances. For me, being the lightweight that I am, that means two drinks; and when I'm one and a half deep, I'm already changing the playlist to Taylor Swift and

Britney and Spice Girls and P!nk, singing along and dancing around the living room. Darcy joins me after her second, and the guys humor us, clapping at the end of every song while they're in the middle of their own conversation.

Soon Darcy and I are in our feels about old crushes thanks to Taylor. We're lying on the couch talking about the guy Darcy dated sophomore year, and the fact that I had a crush on Rafe for three years before he noticed me.

"He belongs with me!" I insist, and Darcy nods seriously.

Suddenly there's movement and Rafe and Alec are on the floor. Wrestling. I don't know if this is part of their conversation or what brought it on, but there's definite tumbling and rolling around. After a couple of minutes Rafe gets Alec on his back, pinning his shoulders to the carpet, and then counts to three and stands up.

"Victory!"

Darcy looks at me. "I feel like I missed something?"

"Yeah. Not that I mind though. That was hot."

"Was it?" Alec asks with a wink, and I nod.

"Would be hotter without shirts on," Darcy points out, and it takes Alec all of half a second to pull his off, showing off his tanned pecs and those angular muscles that disappear under his shorts. My obsession with those muscles borders on unhealthy.

I look at Rafe expectantly and he hesitates for a moment, which makes me want to reassure him that he'll always be my favorite, no matter how cut Alec is.

"You really have to show off those arms," I say. "And the happy trail that always makes me think dirty thoughts."

I must be more drunk than I thought to have said that out loud.

"I promise not to ogle too much," Alec adds. "A little, but not too much."

"Rafe your type?" I ask, grinning.

Alec winks. "Rafe's *everyone's* type."

At that Rafe rolls his eyes and pulls his shirt off, and we all clap. I blow him a kiss and then the guys crouch and start circling each other.

Darcy hops to her feet. "On your mark..." she says, and I have no idea if that's the right terminology for wrestling, but it sounds good. "Get set... go!"

This time it seems to take longer. There are a few times when it seems like Rafe could have pinned Alec but he doesn't, or Alec squirms out from his grip.

It's also way hotter to watch Alec and Rafe half-naked and grabbing at each other, grunting and breathing hard. I scoot closer to Darcy on the couch and she wraps an arm around my shoulder, her skin warm and soft against mine.

"Don't take this the wrong way," I whisper. "But your husband is really fucking hot."

She laughs. This isn't the first time I've said that, though it is the first time I've said it while his naked chest is so close to my husband's.

"You wish you were in the middle of that man sandwich?" she asks, sounding almost jealous.

"He's great to look at, but I'm not interested in anything beyond that," I promise.

She chuckles, stroking my hair. It feels nice, and I rest my head against hers. "Though I would totally record this and watch it on repeat," I say.

"With a vibrator down my pants," she adds.

Fuck. I didn't need that visual: Rafe and Alec grunting and grinding while Darcy gets herself off, making those noises we heard last night. Talk about a fantasy.

I'm unwell at the hotness of it.

Alec finally pins Rafe and Rafe must be tired because it really seems like he should have been able to get out from under him. But he lays there, Alec draped on top of him, chest heaving. After a long moment he puts his hand on Alec's back.

"You got me," he says, and Alec nods but doesn't move. Once they've caught their breath, he slides off him and stands up, reaches a hand down for Rafe, and pulls him to standing.

"I think it's time to go to sleep," Alec says. He throws Darcy a glance I can't fully decode, and she just laughs before standing up to join him.

"See you in the morning!" she says brightly before they disappear into their bedroom, and I try not to think about these new images that have invaded my thoughts. It's not how I'm used to thinking about my best friends, but I'm not sure how to make them go away. I need to figure it out, though, otherwise every comment and every look is going to seem charged, even though it's all in my imagination.

Chapter Six

"THEY'RE TOTALLY GONNA BANG again," I whisper when we enter our room. "I think that's what that glance they exchanged meant, it was fuck-me eyes."

"That's not what Alec's fuck-me eyes look like," Rafe says, as I head into the bathroom for ibuprofen and water.

"Good, I hope not." I take the meds and down some water, then pass him both. "I don't want to spend the whole vacation listening to their late-night smash sessions."

"I thought last night was hot," Rafe says.

"Super hot," I agree. "But it feels weird that they don't know? Voyeuristic. These are our—"

"Best friends, I know," he interrupts. "But you can't always help what you feel about your best friend."

"I guess." I'm too drunk for this conversation. I chug more water in the hopes that the morning won't be miserable. "I just wish we could tell them."

"We *can* tell them," he says, a mischievous glint in his eye, and I laugh.

"What, like go knock on their door and be all: 'if you guys have sex tonight, you should probably know that we can hear it all and we're on the other side of the wall getting off to it?'"

He shakes his head and slips a hand in my underwear. I'm a little disoriented by this subject change, but not against it. Especially since we're still in the bathroom so we can't be overheard.

"Oh, hi," I say with a grin, and instead of replying Rafe just leans in for a kiss. I return it, of course, wrapping my arms around his neck. He starts to move us, but I'm not in the mood to break the kiss, so I just follow his lead, the hand that's cupping my pussy gently guiding me backwards. Then I stop and open my eyes when I feel a wall at my back.

The wall.

He presses himself against me and I feel his hardness against my stomach as he dips his head down. "I think we should fuck right here," he says, mouth against my ear.

My body has an immediate reaction to the suggestion, and Rafe notices—he'd have to, considering where his hand is.

"You like the idea," he says, and I try to breathe through the fact that he's ever so slowly sliding a finger into my pussy.

"They'll hear us!" I whisper back.

He laughs quietly. "That's kind of the point."

His finger is now fully inside me, palm against my clit, and I bite back a groan, resting my forehead against his shoulder.

"This has the potential to make things so awkward," I say.

"Or really fucking hot," Rafe counters, sliding his palm back and forth, and the friction against my clit is so good. Then he pulls his finger out and slowly adds a second. As he slides it in he gets dangerously close to my G-spot, and my breath catches, ending up both relieved and disappointed when he avoids it.

"Tell me to stop and I will," he says, and I kind of hate that he's leaving the decision up to me. The idea of them listening to us and liking it is *unbearably* hot for reasons I don't quite want to dissect right now. I can just picture them on the other side of the wall, fucking in time with the sound of us against the wall like we did last night.

But also, they're our best friends.

Rafe's other hand slips under the shirt of his that I'm wearing to cup one of my breasts lightly. Fuck, it's torture, but the best kind. When he pinches my nipple, I swallow down another groan.

He's being so fucking careful, only playing with the parts of me I can be silent through, and damnit can't he just stroke my G-spot once? Take the decision out of my hands, decide for the both of us that we're going to be loud? But he doesn't.

"Tell me to stop and I will," he says again, and I finally just shake my head and kiss him.

His hand on my breast gets rougher. He pinches my nipple, twists it a bit, and fuck it, I groan.

He pulls back to look at me, surprised, because we both know I could have held that one back but I didn't. I'm glad the dark hides the fact that I'm probably flushed bright red.

"Yeah?" he whispers, but instead of answering with words I pull his head down to me and kiss him and we're off.

The fingers inside me twist, grazing my G-spot and I groan again, letting my head fall back against the wall with a loud thud. He switches back to his thumb against my clit and I put my leg up on the nightstand, spreading myself wider for him. Something tumbles off it—my phone, maybe—and clatters to the ground, but noise is the point, isn't it?

He's hard and I can feel him against my hip, so I slip my hand into his boxers and now it's his turn to groan as I grip his cock. Experience has taught me that if I want him to stay quiet enough so that the kids won't hear, I have to be gentle. So, I do the opposite, tugging harder than usual, and what would normally be a whimper is a loud and sexy-as-fuck grunt.

"You liked that," he says, because my pussy clenched around his fingers when I heard him and I nod, because *obviously*.

Another tug, another grunt, and then he shakes his head. "Now it's your turn."

He smirks in that evil way that suggests he's about to have a lot of fun and pulls my lower half away from the wall so that my top half is leaning against it. But the angle is steep, and I have one foot on the nightstand and the other between his legs so I'm a little unsteady, counting on the fingers in my pussy to help me balance. A forearm comes to rest by my head and he leans forward, looming over me, and for a moment gives me a sweet smile, then a soft kiss.

"Love you," he whispers, and it's quiet enough that I know it's just for me, not for the audience we might have on the other side of the wall.

"Love you too," I whisper back, and in that moment, I feel it. How much I love him, how much I love my life, how lucky I am to have found this man who after fifteen years of marriage still makes my heart pound and my knees weak with just a look. It's almost too much, this contrast between this overwhelming love I'm feeling and the fact that I'm spread open for him with two—nope, now three—fingers in my pussy and my hand around his cock.

And then, with great enthusiasm, he goes after my G-spot.

"Oh fuck," I gasp, caught off guard by the way he's rubbing me, by how quickly the sensation builds. The fingers inside me pull up a bit and now I'm on my tip toes. I couldn't pull away even if I wanted to because he has me and my only option is to ride his hand.

I cry his name, knowing I'm loud because I'm always loud when he does this. But right now I don't even care. "It's so good."

"Fuck yeah it is," he says, and he, too, has stopped whispering. My body again reacts to him because I love dirty talk and we both know it. "Of course it's good, my fingers are always good on you," he says, "You're so fucking wet for me, and in a minute I'm going to stick my cock in you and you'll be wet for that too, won't you?"

I nod, and I've regained enough composure and balance that I can move against his hand, taking an active part in my fucking. But he pulls up enough that I have to stop, at the mercy of his fingers again.

"I'm sorry," he says, and the smirk is back. "I think I asked you a question."

"You did?" I ask, and I honestly don't remember for a moment, the mere idea that he expects me to have my wits about me seems bizarre.

But then. "Right, your cock. Come on, you know I'm wet as fuck right now, you've got three fingers preparing me for you. And I'm ready, I'm *so* ready, please just fuck me already? Please?"

I'm begging now, because that's what Rafe does to me, makes me want more until all I can do is beg and plead and hope that he'll give me the release that I need. His fingers are amazing and they work a special kind of magic, but sometimes I just ache for his cock, for the connection we get when he's inside me.

"I want it, I want *you* so bad."

He grins and pulls his fingers out, and I sag against the wall, breathing hard.

"Bed," he says, and I scramble there. But when I lay down, he shakes his head and flips me over, shifting me to my hands and knees, placing me where he wants. He leans me forward, wrapping my fingers around the top of the headboard, then kisses his way down my back before settling behind me.

And then, for a moment, we both just look at the wall.

They may not even be there. Maybe they're out for a walk, or decided to go skinny dipping in the ocean like Alec had joked about earlier.

And even if they had been there, they might have left as soon as they heard us start. It would be the polite thing to do. The thoughtful thing to do. What we probably should have done, instead of getting all hot and bothered and having amazingly intense sex.

It's very possible we're just doing this for ourselves.

I look over my shoulder at Rafe, and he mouths, *You good?*

I nod, and then mouth, *Love you.*

A look of tenderness comes over his face and he leans forward and closes the distance between us for a kiss.

"Love you too," he whispers, then kisses my shoulder. And then, against my ear, "I'm going to fuck you now, if that's okay."

I laugh and nod and then gasp as he slides into me slowly. "Fuck," I whisper, and he thrusts from behind, leaning over me. He palms my breasts and then focuses on my nipples. I muffle my noises against my arm, being quiet because that's my natural state.

Because they might not even be there, so now this is for us, not as part of a show. It's us fucking how we fuck, mostly quietly with the occasional loud noise and just the right amount of banter.

Approaching two decades together means that he knows me and can tell when I'm about to come, so he stops just short of my orgasm, and I know I'm in for a long night. I whine, because I always do, and he laughs, flipping me over so that he can go down on me.

He's at the foot of the bed, laying on his side, and I relax as his tongue plays with my clit, explores my folds. His fingers are where his real talent lies, but his tongue is lovely and after a minute it's so fucking good.

But I can't fully relax, so I try to shift my upper body closer to him while not disrupting him. It doesn't work, and he pulls away, leaving my pussy wet and cold and exposed to the air.

"What do you want, woman?" he asks with a mouth that's glistening with my juices, but there's a hint of a grin, because he knows exactly what I want.

"Gimme your dick," I say, and motion for him to swing his body around.

He rolls his eyes as if making himself available is some kind of great favor to me, but adjusts, and when I wrap my mouth around his cock he groans. Then he goes after my clit again, and we race to see who can make the other person come first.

I'm about to win, but then he pulls away, and we both lay there for a moment, trying to catch our breath. He's rubbing my clit gently but it's not enough to get me anywhere. Aside from the frustration of not being able to come, this feels lovely and exquisite while we rest up for the next round.

"Stop trying to make me come before I'm ready," he growls once he's recovered, crawling over to me while I laugh and adjust my position, grabbing a pillow and handing it to him.

"Stop pulling away when I'm about to come," I counter, as he wraps an arm around my ass and pulls my lower half off the bed, sliding the pillow under my hips and leaning over me, pulling my legs up over his shoulders.

"Promise I'll let you this time," he says, and I grin, because I know this game and that he hasn't decided it's time yet.

But this position means his cock strokes my G-spot, so even if he doesn't do it quite enough for a full orgasm it's really fucking good. My body is right on the edge. I want the release so badly, and I start moving more, trying to get myself there. I reach down for my clit but he seizes my hand and pins it above my head.

"You'll come when I'm good and ready for you to come," he says, then pulls out of me completely.

I wrench my hand free of him and pull another pillow to cover my face with it. My body is so primed, and I need this orgasm so bad. "You're the worst!"

He grins into the crook of my neck. "I'm the best."

I lift the pillow to look at him, kneeling over me—the cock and chest and shoulders and arms and gorgeous face that I get to see every morning.

He's right, he *is* the best.

I cross my arms over my chest, pushing my tits up. "Says the guy who can't even make me come."

Now the grin that crosses his face is a bit wicked, and I know I'm about to get my orgasm.

"Oh, now you're asking for it. Watch yourself, Rebecca, because I'm going to prove you wrong," he says.

He leans down to kiss me as I laugh into his mouth. And we fuck again, starting off slow, but then we build speed and strength. He knows the moves that work, he knows how to slip his hand between us and how to touch my clit. His cock strokes my G-spot and his finger is massaging my clit and the coil in me tightens, and I know this one's it, this is the time we're both going to come. He's getting close too, and I want us to come at the same time, so I do my best to hold off even though my body is begging for release, *screaming* for it.

I wrap my arms around his shoulder and gasp against his skin and he whispers how much he loves me and how gorgeous I am and how I'm everything and it's almost too much and we're both right there. And then it happens. My body snaps and my pussy clenches, squeezing him, and he can feel it because he freezes, deep inside me. It's all too good, it's too much, it's everything, it's Rafe. I both can't stand it and want more of it because it'll never be enough with him.

Then he sags against me, pinning me to the bed, and pressing a kiss to my temple.

"Love you," he whispers, and I whisper it back.

And that's when we hear a thud in the room next door and Darcy's voice say, "Shit."

Chapter Seven

"I'M NOT LEAVING," I insist, holding the covers more tightly over my head even as Rafe tries to pull them off. "Tell them I'm hungover and need the morning to recover."

It wouldn't be hard to believe, seeing as I do have a headache and we didn't wake up until nine. Which, when you have three children, is definitely considered sleeping in. We kept the shades tightly drawn until we heard Alec and Darcy banging around the kitchen (not actually banging, just making a racket) which was around 9:30. So they, too, were slow to rise. But that was an hour ago.

Rafe stops tugging and then I feel him slide next to me, tangling our legs together and pulling me closer to him. "So you'll come out by afternoon?"

"No, but this'll buy me some time to come up with the next excuse."

Rafe laughs, but it's indulgent more than anything, and the covers shift around as he comes into view, backlit by the sun filtering through the sheets. He's naked, a little damp from his shower, and looks mouthwatering. I let my gaze travel over him slowly, lingering at his cock, which is—exactly how we got in this mess in the first place.

"They heard us have sex!"

"Yes, but we knew that was going to happen," he points out.

"I know, but I got distracted and forgot."

He grins, shifting closer to me. "Was it my dick? Was that what got you so distracted?"

"Maybe," I say, cracking a smile.

He nudges his nose against mine and presses a quick kiss to my mouth. "I forgot too," he admits.

"So let's just stay in here forever so we never have to face them?"

He rolls on his side, propping himself up with one arm. "Staying in bed all day is hardly the best way to distract them from thinking about us having sex. Plus, they're our ride home."

I bury my face in his chest and he wraps an arm around my waist, holding me for a minute.

"Darcy knows you, mi vida. If she figures out we knew what we were doing—and that's a big if—she knows we were drunk. She also probably knows that you're dying of embarrassment inside. And as much as she loves teasing you, she'll let this one go without too much torture."

He's right, I know this, but still. "I think part of it is that I feel bad for making them listen to us."

"They could have left," he points out. "The same way we could have the night before. If they stayed..."

He doesn't finish the sentence, but the next words are obvious. If they stayed it's probably because they liked it. Every time I consider that possibility, my whole body flushes. Because I want to know. Did they get off listening to us get off? Were we as hot as they were the night before?

Should I even be thinking these things about our best friends?

Rafe always knows exactly what to ask, and he lightly taps my head. "Tell me what you've got going on up there?"

I bury my face into his chest again as he runs his fingers through my hair. "This is just equal parts weird, and..."

I don't want to say it because it's so awkward to admit, but he finishes the sentence for me.

"Hot."

I nod against his skin and he's patient, the fingers in my hair soothing. Finally, I take a deep breath and pull away.

"Okay, it's fine. It's going to be fine! We're adults, and you're right, Darcy won't say anything. I'm good."

"Ready for breakfast?" he asks, and my nod is more confident than I feel.

***

When we emerge fifteen minutes later, Darcy and Alec are at the bar in the kitchen, heads bent together and speaking quietly. She pulls away when we walk in and smiles nervously at us.

"Morning, sleepyhead."

"Morning," I say, heading straight for the coffee pot and pouring myself a cup. Maybe caffeine will make things feel a little more normal.

"Alec made some bacon, it's next to the stove. And bread's right next to the toaster."

"Thanks," I say, trying to be casual about the fact that I'm avoiding looking at them, engrossed in preparing my toast and serving myself some bacon. I take the spot next to Darcy and she reaches over and squeezes my arm.

"You okay?" she asks quietly, and I take a deep breath and nod.

"Yeah. You?"

She wraps an arm around my shoulders and gives me a squeeze, resting her head against mine. "Golden."

Rafe sits next to me and gives my knee a squeeze. Sandwiched between my two favorite people in the world, I relax a little. I'm fine. It's fine.

"So what's the plan for today, then?"

The answer is more beach, so we change into our suits and walk the two blocks there. The good thing about coming to South Padre in September is that it's still stupid hot, but it's almost empty because kids are in school. An attempt at boogie boarding results in me almost losing my top, so I head back to the blanket and lay out, letting the sun dry me off. A few minutes later Darcy joins me. When she walks up all wet and dripping I can only look at her for half a second before I roll over on my stomach. It's like I'm seventeen again and totally crushing on my best friend.

Except this isn't a crush, just a deep awareness of her body. Totally different.

"Had enough?" I ask, folding my arms and resting my head on them, facing her direction but not looking right at her.

She nods, lying down in a pose that mirrors mine. "Serious wipe out. If I'd been wearing a two-piece I'd definitely be walking back topless."

I let out a choked laugh, forcing the image of Darcy walking towards me—pink, laughing, and topless, barely covering her boobs with her arm—out of my mind.

No, seriously, *what* is wrong with me?

"Are we just going to come to the beach every day?" she asks. "I mean, not that I'm complaining. I'm definitely down for it, just wondering."

"There's some other stuff we can do," I say, thinking back to the list of activities I'd found online. "A few walks and hikes. We can check out the sand dunes which could be a fun place for Alec to flex his photography skills. Oh, and horseback riding."

Darcy grins, flicking her hand like she's cracking a whip. "I'll pass on the horses. I want to get my fill of a different kind of riding this week, if you know what I mean."

It's the kind of comment that would normally make me laugh, but today my face flushes hot and I'm sure it's bright red.

"I didn't mean—" she starts, then groans, burying her face in her arms.

"I know, I know!" I say.

She turns her head halfway, peeking at me with one eye. "Are we talking about this, or not?"

"I'd really rather not."

She takes a deep breath and nods. "Okay, then you have to let me make sex jokes without assuming I'm thinking about you guys."

I nod, trying not to think about her thinking about us.

Trying not to think about them, and what we heard the first night.

"Deal. And also, no horses. Save up your energy for Alec."

Darcy props herself up on her elbows and I follow her gaze to the ocean where Rafe and Alec are.

"We really lucked out with those two, didn't we?" she says.

I nod. "We really did."

***

Now that we've discussed the fact that we aren't going to discuss it, things feel less awkward. By the time we leave the beach I'm not really self-conscious about the whole thing. We're adults, we know we're all having sex, it's fine.

Originally, we'd planned on a nearby food truck park for dinner, but we're so exhausted from the beach that we decide to have a low-key night at the rental instead. We make sandwiches and lay around the living room watching a movie, but around 8pm we get a second wind and decide to break in the hot tub.

My swimsuit is still damp when I pull it on, and goosebumps pop up all over my skin from the combination of the wet suit and the AC. Apparently, that's not all that pops up though, because Rafe does a double take and then breaks into a grin.

"What?" I ask, rubbing my palms on my arms to warm up. Instead of answering he spins me around so that I'm facing the bathroom mirror.

"Oh."

My swimsuit lining doesn't hide the fact that my nipples have gone hard.

"Fucking hot," he says, tugging my top down so a breast pops out. "God, I love your tits."

"Perv."

But the way I watch him makes it obvious that I like his perviness. His fingers brush lightly against the puckered nipple, and I feel it getting even harder, my skin tightening under his hand. He frees the other tit and we watch as he just plays with me. Something prods at my lower back, and I grin at him in the mirror.

"Like anyone in their right mind would blame me," he says, and then groans softly as I wiggle, putting pressure against his erection.

He ducks his head down so that his mouth is right next to my ear. "Tease."

"Yep," I say with a grin, and he pinches my nipples in response. My whole body jerks and I bite down on my lip to keep from making a noise. He does it again, and again, and my clit starts to pulse even though it hasn't even been touched.

"Rafe," I finally gasp, and he chuckles against my ear.

In retaliation I reach behind me, cupping his cock over his pants, and he presses himself into my hand. I grin at him in the mirror, and he rocks against me as he plays with my tits.

Suddenly, I hear Darcy's voice, way too close.

"You guys coming or not?"

"Shit!" I whisper, tucking myself back into my swimsuit, and then call out, "Yep, just a sec!"

There's not nearly enough time to hide my nipples, but I tug at my suit anyway, hoping they're not obvious.

When I step out of the bathroom Darcy's right in the doorway of our room, looking at something on her phone. But when she glances up, she looks me up and down, and a knowing smile crosses her face.

"What?" I ask, hoping she's smiling about something else.

Her smile widens. "Has anyone told you that you're really cute when you're turned on?"

"Shut up." My face heats up, but she's Darcy, so of course she keeps going.

"You're all flushed—not just your face, but also your chest—and you're super flustered, which is adorable. And the way you've turned those headlights on?" She kisses her fingertips with a flourish. "Makes those tits of yours even more outstanding."

"Shut up," I say again, turning to the mirror above the dresser and pulling my hair into a ponytail. She's right though, my face and chest are pink, and my nipples are impossible to ignore. It's obvious she interrupted something.

I glare at the mirror, pulling my hair down and putting it up again, to distract my mind from going back, again and again, to Darcy calling me cute.

"See, that's the adorably flustered thing I love. I swear, if I wasn't married..."

"Are you hitting on my wife?"

Rafe appears at the doorway of the bathroom, looking more put together than I am. Did he rub one out super quick, or just think unsexy things? He's wearing his swimsuit but no shirt, and it reminds me why I need to stop thinking about Darcy. I've already got someone I'm completely in love with, and to want anything more would just be too much.

"Don't worry, only hypothetically," Darcy says lightly, leaning against the door. "Since we're both married, it'll have to stay a fantasy."

"If you want a hall pass so you can hook up with Darcy, I could be convinced," Rafe says, eyes twinkling as he meets my gaze in the mirror, as if he can read my thoughts. But I know it's a joke, so I roll my eyes.

"Provided I can watch," he adds with a smirk that sends my mind to a dozen dirty places where my limbs are tangled with Darcy's and Rafe watches, dick in his hand.

"I hate you both," I say, though the words lack any kind of bite. After making a big deal of shaking my head, I push past Darcy to go to the hot tub, but she reaches out and catches my hand. When I glance at her she looks at me questioningly and gives my hand a squeeze.

We good? is the implied question.

I roll my eyes again, but make it playful, and squeeze her hand back with a nod. Because of course we are—I can't imagine a world where we're anything else. When Rafe approaches the door she drops my hand, letting me go.

"She's also got great legs," Rafe stage-whispers to Darcy.

"Oh, trust me, I've noticed," Darcy whispers back.

Chapter Eight

WE TURN OUT THE porch lights to keep the bugs away, and the full moon lights our way. The outside air is warm, but the ocean breeze keeps things cool. When I slip into the hot tub the water caresses my skin. The others join me, and the moonlight makes everyone even more attractive than usual, casting enough of a spell over us that I have to look away and study the shadows of the trees and houses.

I normally wouldn't drink two nights in a row, but there's something about tonight that makes me want to take the edge off, so I accept the beer Alec offers. Two nights of hearing each other through the walls, of grunts and sighs and groans that at this point we all know the other couple heard, has left tension that's easier to ignore during the day than it is at night.

Still, we try, as Darcy and I gossip about *The Bachelor* and Rafe and Alec have their standard Spurs vs Lakers banter.

"Have they ever had a queer season?" Alec asks when the sports discussion is done, and I shake my head.

"One of the leads came out later, and there have been a few bi contestants, but never a queer lead while it was on."

"And it feels like they're always playing up the bi contestants for drama, as opposed to them just being...I don't know"—Darcy shrugs—"them."

"I don't know how much my opinion counts," I say. It's my constant dilemma as a bi woman who's only ever been with men. "But I wish there was more bi rep on TV that just... was. Instead of it being a whole thing."

"Why don't you count?" Alec asks.

"Because Rafael scooped her up before she got a chance to play around with the ladies," Darcy answers. I grab Rafe's hand and wrap it around my shoulders, leaning against him.

"He's a pretty okay consolation prize," I tease, looking up at him, and he presses a kiss on my hairline with a distracted smile.

"Do you regret not having had the chance?" Alec asks, showing more interest in this than I'd have expected, but the answer is easy.

"Regret? Nah. I'm curious, sure, but I'd rather have Rafe now than miss out on him just to have that experience. It's kind of like how I feel about..." I glance at Rafe, trying to think of something equivalent.

"A threesome?" he asks, because that was a discussion we had a few months ago.

I laugh and nod. "Yeah, exactly. Curiosity and active desire are two different things."

"Alec had a threesome in college," Darcy says, and both my and Rafe's eyes swing around to him.

"Wait what?" Rafe asks, while I add, "How have we never heard about this before?"

"Two guys, one girl," Darcy says, as Alec looks an impressive mix of arrogant and self-conscious. "I'm forever jealous of her."

I reach for my beer and take a swig as fortification. "I'm going to need details."

Alec laughs, then shrugs. "What kind of details?"

I look at Darcy because she knows what I'm asking, and she laughs. "They made out."

"Like a three-way kiss?"

"We took turns," Alec cuts in.

"And they all went down on each other."

"Taking turns *then* all at the same time in a triangle," Alec says with a bit of a smirk, and I play at fanning myself.

"And then DP." Darcy shakes her head. "*So* fucking jealous."

"You have a double penetration fantasy?" I ask, though I'm not sure why it surprises me. I know she and Alec have anal sex—it's a more recent addition to their repertoire. She'd told me about it back when it was just a discussion of something they might try. I guess if I were into anal, and had a threesome with Rafe and another guy, I'd want to try DP. But those are two big ifs—for one, Rafe and I have never tried anal. Second, even though we've talked about threesomes, it's always in a theoretical way. I think we're both afraid of getting jealous, and even if that wasn't a factor it would be hard to find someone that would work.

I also don't even know *how* to find someone.

"Fuck yes," Darcy says. "We've played around with toys since we're not going to bring another dude into our bedroom, but God, if I were single—sorry, TMI?"

"A little," Rafe says in a choked voice, and I glance up at him, realizing that he hasn't said anything this entire conversation. And, not for the first time this week, I wonder if he also has a bit of a crush on Darcy.

The idea makes me uncomfortable—jealous, even, which is another tick in the 'no threesome' column. Though, to be honest, my jealousy is about both of them. I know that doesn't make any sense—for one, if I can be trusted with a crush on her, so can he. We've talked about crushes before, she shouldn't be any different.

But for whatever reason my crush on her *does* feel different than other crushes I've had. My attraction to Alec doesn't go beyond wanting to watch him do basically anything with his shirt off, or maybe fuck Darcy, but the idea that Rafe might want to do more than just watch Darcy...

Whatever, it's fine. No one's acting on feelings for anyone.

Alec's voice cuts through my thoughts. "If you had the opportunity to hook up with a chick, would you?"

"You don't have to answer that," Darcy cuts in, sending Alec a look I can't quite interpret, and I shrug.

"I'm not about to put my marriage at risk, so it's a non-issue."

"But what if I were okay with it?" Rafe asks, and I look at him again. Wonder if he's thinking about me and Darcy. Fuck now *I'm* thinking about me and Darcy. "If I could be there, I could be okay with it," he adds.

"Such a dude," I say with a grin, rolling my eyes.

But he surprises me when he says, "I don't mean watching in a pervy way. Like, yeah, there's some voyeurism involved, but there's also some... I don't know. Watching you orgasm? That's always hot. Watching someone who appreciates what a fucking goddess you are? They better! But watching you explore this part of yourself that you haven't before..." he shrugs. "I think it would be cool. Then again, it could be weird intruding on a private moment..."

His voice wavers with uncertainty, and I cut in. "No, I'd want you there. I mean, you're my husband, having a sexual experience without you there would be awkward, maybe feel wrong? And since I realized I was bi, since I came out to you, you've always been really supportive of that side of me. I think having you there would be nice." I flush. "Not that I'm going to be hooking up with anyone other than you anytime soon."

He chuckles, and I wrap my hand around his neck, pulling him down for a kiss.

"Love you," he says quietly.

"Love you too."

"A-hem," Darcy says, exaggeratingly loud, and I flush, pressing my face into Rafe's chest. We're all laughing, though.

I flick her off, and then settle against Rafe again, wrapping his arm around my waist. "So I guess my answer is maybe? In the right circumstance I could see it. No idea how you end up in that situation but..." I shrug. "Sure, in theory. How about you guys? Darcy, I know you've been with a woman before."

"We only made out and groped a little. I don't think it counts if there's nothing under the clothing."

"It counts," Alec says, wrapping his arm around her shoulders, and I nod in agreement.

"Would you? Or how would you feel about Alec hooking up with someone else?"

They look at each other thoughtfully. "I don't know how I'd feel about you hooking up with a woman," Darcy says, and Alec nods.

"I kind of want to be the only cock you fuck," he agrees, and now it's Rafe's turn to cut in.

"Okay, but that's different than not wanting her with another man," he says. "There's plenty of sex stuff that doesn't involve cocks, and people of all genders that may or may not have one."

Alec is quiet for a moment, pursing his lips. He tilts his head to the side as he considers Rafe's comment, finally answering, "True... maybe I think I'd have to make the decision in the moment? Maybe it's less about their gender, and more about the specific person. Whether or not I feel like they could replace me."

Darcy's face softens as she looks over at him. "No one could replace you," she says, and he grins and gives her a kiss.

I look over at Rafe, expecting to exchange glances at how cute our friends are, but instead see him looking hesitant. Anxious.

"You okay?" I ask.

He looks down at me, tightening his arms around my waist and swallowing. "What if I hooked up with someone else?"

I feel a wave of guilt at my answer, because it comes to me easily. "I don't think so," I admit. "I'm already jealous thinking of you with another woman."

Rafe opens his mouth as if to say something, then closes it again. He's watching me, serious, and I know there's something he isn't saying. Curious, I give his leg a little squeeze, and he takes a deep breath. Darcy and Alec tilt their heads together, talking quietly. They're doing their best to give him some privacy, because it's obvious to all of us that there's something just under the surface.

He clears his throat, and finally asks, "What about someone who wasn't a woman?"

Darcy and Alec stop whispering, and all three of us look at him because he's straight. He's always said so. He jokes about being the token straight amongst three bisexuals.

I glance at Darcy, who appears curious when her eyes meet mine, and then at Alec, who actually doesn't look all that surprised. And then I look back at Rafe, who quickly adds, "We're just talking hypothetically, of course."

And that's when I know he is, at the very least, bi-curious, and more than likely some flavor of queer. Realizing that–or at least acknowledging it–at thirty-eight is probably a bit of a mind fuck. I lace our fingers together and give his hand a squeeze.

But also, now I get what he meant about how he'd love to watch me explore a different side of myself. Because I can't help him understand what it means to be bi, but if it was something he was really interested in playing around with, I'd want to be there.

And then I think of what it would be like to be present when he is in a vulnerable place, experimenting and trying to figure out who he is and what he likes. I imagine him experiencing that for the first time, fucking or getting fucked, and how much of a privilege it would be to see it, if he would be comfortable with that.

And suddenly the question becomes less complicated, and the answer more clear. It's not about him having sex with someone else, it's about him getting to experience the full range of his sexuality.

"Yeah," I say, then grin. "And if you wanted me to be there, I'd be honored."

He kisses me, and whispers, "I would."

I shift to my knees, facing him and one of his hands slides up my back, cradling the back of my neck, while the other grabs my ass, pulling me against him. I can feel him hardening against my thigh and really all I want to do is pull my suit to the side and slide down on him, let him know how lucky I am to be with him. To be with someone who's open and honest and vulnerable and hot as fuck. I want to make him come a dozen times and that still won't express how he makes me feel.

It takes a minute for me to remember that we have an audience. When I do, I pull away, breathing heavily, and rest my forehead against his.

"They're watching us, aren't they," I ask in a stage-whisper, and he grins.

"Probably."

"I'm really grumpy we can't have sex tonight."

Then Darcy pipes in, "You can. Just know that if you do, we're on the other side of the wall."

"Getting off to it," Alec adds.

That turns me on way more than it should. My whole body flushes. I try to play it off, pressing my face into Rafe's neck and laughing in the hopes that they can't see how affected I am. Hoping they can't tell that now I want to go jump in bed and have loud sex because I'm pretty sure knowing they're listening and doing the same will only make it hotter.

"TMI!" I say, face hidden in Rafe's chest, and he's shaking against me with laughter as well.

"Whatever," Darcy says. "We know you did it the first night."

Just when I thought I couldn't get more embarrassed. Or turned on. Or... whatever this jumble of feelings I'm having is. I stop laughing and turn my head slightly towards them, peeking through my fingers.

"I have no idea what you're talking about."

"It's fine," Alec insists. "It's not a big deal, we're all adults. Plus, you guys were roommates in college. Hooking up with someone while your roommate's asleep on the top bunk is basically a rite of passage."

"We didn't do that," I tell him, but when I look at Darcy she's avoiding my gaze. "Wait, seriously?"

"You're a heavy sleeper! Besides, you would have done it too, except you barely had a sex life in college!"

I shake my finger at her. "Not true! I had a sex life, it was just long-distance the first year and junior year, the guy had a single. And then Rafe had an apartment. How often were you hooking up with people while I was in the room?"

"It doesn't matter, it's in the past!" she insists, and I look at Rafe to share a 'what the fuck' moment, but he's looking guilty and refusing to meet my eye.

"Seriously? Am I the only person who's never been an exhibitionist?"

"Until last night," Darcy points out, and the guys laugh while I just splash some water in her direction.

We head to bed for the night shortly after.

"Tomorrow we can come up with a sex schedule or something," I say, and Alec chuckles.

"Prude," Darcy says, but I know she's teasing and when we step out of the hot tub she pulls me into a hug, wrapping her arms around my shoulders as I wrap mine around her waist.

She's warm from the hot tub, and the contrast between that and the chilly night air feels good against my skin. Damp, too. There's nothing about this moment I don't like. The hug lingers a few beats longer than usual. I don't want to let go, but thankfully the beer has mostly worn off at this point so I don't do anything I'll regret.

When I do finally pull away, I grab my towel and Alec wraps Darcy up with him in his. He says something I can't hear but it makes her look as loved up as I've seen her. Her hands go up to his face and she pulls him down for a kiss. Then I read her lips as she tells him she loves him.

I glance at Rafe, who's watching them too, and I suspect we're thinking the same thing.

"Twenty minutes?" I whisper.

He shakes his head. "Thirty."

"You think you can keep me busy for thirty?" I tease. He laughs and wiggles his eyebrows.

I turn back to Darcy and Alec. "Hey, so Rafe and I are going to, um—"

"Take a shower," Rafe cuts in with a grin. "For half an hour. Which means we won't be in our room for that stretch of time. So if you—"

"Got it!" Darcy calls and grabs Alec's hand to drag him inside as Rafe and I laugh.

Chapter Nine

Rafe turns the shower on as soon as we get in the bathroom, and it's steaming by the time we're out of our suits and stepping inside. Wrapping his arms around my waist, he pulls me to him, but the kiss he gives me is gentle.

"Do we need to talk?" he asks, a little hesitant.

I shake my head. "We don't need to, no. If you *want* to, we can. But if you don't, we don't have to, tonight or any other night."

He runs his hands through my hair, which is quickly getting wet under the flow of water, and then kisses me again.

"I've never actually said it," he says.

"Do you want to?"

He takes a deep breath, as if he's about to, then wrinkles his nose. "Am I making too big a deal about this? It feels like it shouldn't matter, I barely even—"

I interrupt him. "I swear to God, Rafe, you've spent the last dozen years telling me I count. If you say you don't, I'm going to kick your ass."

He laughs. "Okay, okay. I count."

"You do."

He readjusts the nozzles so that they spray the bench at the back of the shower and then sits down, pulling me into his lap. I curl up against him, wrapping my arms around his neck.

"It doesn't weird you out?" he asks, and I shake my head. "Or make me seem less...I don't know."

I'm patient, waiting for him to say whatever he's thinking because I can tell he does know, he's just not saying it.

"When we met I was this athletic soccer player, a ladies' man. I'd like to think I'm still a little athletic and a bit of a ladies' man, even if it's just for you."

I chuckle and nod. "You're definitely still both of these things."

"So does finding this out make me less..." He hesitates again. Swallows. "Masculine, I guess? Manly?"

It's not that I *want* him to be insecure, but every time he shows me that he is, I melt a little more. The vulnerability and trust involved in him letting me see that side of him captivates me.

I give him a smile and shake my head. "Does anything about Alec seem less masculine to you?"

He doesn't answer, but he does flush, which happens so rarely that it takes a minute for everything to click.

"Wait," I say. "Oh my God."

He makes a real effort to not meet my eyes, and I stand up.

"You don't have a crush on Darcy?"

This makes him look at me. "What? No. Of course I don't have a crush on your best friend."

A slow grin crosses my face. "You have a crush on her husband. On *your* best friend!"

"He's not my best friend," Rafe says, grumpy. "Nate is my best friend, but he lives in Minnesota so Alec's just my best friend in the geographic area."

I hardly hear his clarification, though. Putting my hands over my heart, I say, "Oh, honey..."

"Shut up," he says, still bright red, and I crawl back into his lap and press a kiss to his cheek.

"I will if you want me to," I say, and he just rolls his eyes.

So I don't say anything for a moment while I process this, because there's been so much tonight. Rafe is bi and crushing on Alec and...

That's when I remember Alec's reaction to Rafe's question. "Does he know?"

"Does who know what?"

"Does Alec know? That you're... whatever on him."

"What? No! Wait, what?" he looks a little panicked, which I get. It's the reaction I'd have if I thought Darcy knew about my crush.

I try to temper my answer. "He just... didn't look surprised when you asked how I'd feel if you hooked up with a guy. Like, at all. But maybe he just had, I don't know, bi-dar."

"Maybe. God, I hope that's all."

"I'm sure it is," I say, pressing a kiss to the center of his chest.

But he doesn't seem convinced, and his leg starts jiggling anxiously. "Oh shit, did I fuck everything up?"

"What? No!" I cup his chin to make him look at me. "Why would you think that?"

"If he knows, it'll just be so awkward."

I can't help it, I laugh.

"What?" he asks.

"Isn't that what this entire trip has been? One horned up, hormonal, awkward, fuckfest?"

"I think I saw that on Pornhub," he says, and I take the fact that he's making a joke as a good sign.

"But seriously. Wouldn't it be awkward if you found out that Darcy was crushing on you or something?" he says.

I consider the question, and awkward definitely isn't what I feel. "No," I say, and my face grows hot.

"No?" he asks.

Going for a joke feels the least risky. "I mean, maybe for like thirty seconds. Then I'd remember tonight, that you and Alec are both cool with it if we hook up, so I'd jump her and let you two watch."

He looks thoughtful for a moment, and I shove his shoulder gently. "It's a joke! But seriously, I can't imagine you and Alec being an issue."

"You sound very sure," he says.

I nod and start ticking off the reasons on my fingers. "First, he's hot, so I doubt this is the first time he's had a friend that's attracted to him.

"Second, you're hot, so I'd be shocked if the idea never crossed his mind. Who wouldn't want to get down with"—I gesture at his body with my hand and he grins, leaning forward to kiss me briefly—"Third, you're both in marriages that, all jokes aside, are monogamous.

"Fourth, you're married to best friends who are very glad their husbands get along, and we'd kick the ass of anyone who screwed up this dynamic.

"And fifth, if it ends up that I'm wrong and it makes our dynamic all wonky"—I shrug—"we'll still be okay."

He studies me, eyes tracing my face with care and tenderness. Now sopping, my hair is mostly plastered to me—I'm in a shower after all—but he pushes it behind my shoulder anyway. Then he kisses me so softly and sweetly that it reminds me of the first time he kissed me: outside my dorm after walking me home from the library, seventeen years ago.

"Love you," he says quietly, and I smile.

"Love you too."

He takes a deep breath. "Would you want to?"

"Want to what?"

His fingers pull a lock of hair back forward again, rubbing it. His eyes go there as well, and I know he's avoiding me, but I don't push it.

"Kiss a woman? More than kiss a woman?" he asks.

It wasn't the question I was expecting, and my head says I should answer no or deflect and ask if he wants to kiss a guy. But he's been vulnerable with me tonight, I owe him honesty, so I take a second to seriously consider the question.

"I don't know? I mean obviously I think about it, we've talked about that. But if I had the opportunity to, and I knew you were okay with it? Maybe? I really don't know though. That's not just me avoiding the answer, it depends. On the woman, on the situation, on a lot of things. Why do you ask?"

He shrugs, still watching his fingers. "I've been thinking about it a lot. Well, I've been thinking about me a lot, but after this trip—after tonight—I've been wondering about you, too."

"And when you think about you," I ask, hoping he knows it's a question borne out of curiosity rather than judgment. "What do you think?"

"That the idea of it is scary as fuck," he says, but then a long beat passes before he finally looks up at me. "But also, really hot. I'm still undecided on whether the hotness outweighs the scariness, though."

I reach out to take his hand, lacing our fingers together. "Maybe we should make a plan to revisit the conversation in a month or two? See what we're thinking? Because I meant what I said earlier, if you decided you really wanted to explore this side of you, I could be open to it?"

He gives my fingers a squeeze. "I meant it, too. With the disclaimer that if after you do it one time it and feels weird or off or wrong then I get to change my mi—"

"Of course." I nod. "No yes is ever a yes forever."

"Then yeah, I'd be fine with you making out—or more—with a woman."

I flush, whole body heating at the idea of 'or more.' God I'd love to go down on a woman. Take everything I've learned after being on the receiving end of Rafe's tongue and try it out on some gorgeous woman who's wriggling and sighing and gasping and asking for more and calling my name. Tasting her and feeling her and knowing she's wet because of me.

Rafe chuckles and I look up at him. "You got this horned-out faraway look in your eyes. We'll definitely revisit it."

I refuse to let myself feel embarrassed, because it's Rafe and there aren't shameful things between us, so I just nod.

Then the subject drifts onto other things—kids and work and tv and movies—and before we know it the water is running cold.

"Holy shit!" I say when we're out of the shower, wrapped in towels. "We were in there for an hour."

Rafe holds his hands up to show off his raisined fingertips. "Oops?"

"What are the odds they're still having sex?" I ask, reaching for my underwear, but Rafe plucks it out of my hand and puts it back on the bathroom counter.

"I bet they're done," he says, but instead of heading to the bedroom he drapes a towel over my head and dries my hair. I close my eyes, enjoying the feel of it, and then of his lips against the crown of my head. Once we're mostly dry, he shepherds us into the bedroom.

Sure enough, the room on the other side of the wall is quiet. Rafe pulls back the covers, gesturing for me to get in.

I do, slipping between the sheets, and then Rafe curls up behind me, making sure every inch of the back of me is pressed against the front of him, skin to skin, all the way down.

"We forgot to have sex," I say, threading my fingers with his, and bringing them up to my mouth for a kiss.

I feel his shoulders raise and lower behind me in a shrug. "I don't think I needed it tonight. What we did was perfect, honestly."

I glance over my shoulder at him and he presses a kiss against my mouth. "I'm glad you told me," I say quietly.

"I'm glad I did too," he admits. "And to make up for no sex I guarantee at least two orgasms tomorrow."

I chuckle, but the truth is, even without sex, the shower was pretty perfect as it was.

Chapter Ten

When I wake up the next morning, for once on this trip, I don't feel awkward. Rafe is still conked out, and while I seriously consider giving him a good-morning blowjob, in the end he looks so peaceful that I don't want to wake him. Instead, I slip out of the covers and try not to disturb him. Pulling on a discarded shirt of his and a pair of pajama shorts, I pad out to the kitchen.

The coffee is almost done brewing when Darcy joins me and I only glance up for a second before turning my attention back to the coffee pot.

"Your pajama game is strong," I say.

"This little thing?"—she gestures to the silky tank top and shorts number that highlights her cleavage and the body underneath—"You flatter me."

I pour a cup of coffee for each of us. and when I turn to her, she's studying me. If I didn't know better, I'd think there was heat in her eyes.

I do know her better, though, so it's definitely not that.

"You're pulling off the 'wearing my husband's clothes because I went to sleep naked' thing very well. Way harder to look sexy in an oversized shirt and a messy bun than in satin and lace."

"Shut up," I say, because she's just teasing, just having fun. If she knew how much time over the past few days I've been thinking about her naked, she'd back off the playful comments a bit.

I busy myself with the pancake mix and start preparing breakfast. After the first pancake is on the griddle, I feel eyes on me. I glance over at her, not quite able to read the expression on her face.

"What?"

"Nothing," she says, with a shake of her head, and now there's something almost sad about her smile. "Thanks for the sex last night."

I chuckle and turn back to the pancakes. "You're welcome." I know I shouldn't say anything more, but I can't help myself, so I ask, "Good?"

"Really good. I swear, Alec is as good with his tongue as you say Rafe is with his hands. And we're back on an anal kick lately. And fuck, his dick is just so good."

"Mmmhmm," I say, trying not to think about where Alec uses his tongue, about how I want to replace his tongue with mine. Trying not to wonder what Darcy looks like and feels like and tastes like.

"You thinking about Rafe?" she asks, and I glance over at her.

"No. Why?"

"Well, you're thinking about *something* sexy because your nipples just started poking out of your shirt."

"Oh, God, Darcy, stop staring at my chest!" I say, pulling the shirt away from my tits and hoping she assumes the flush is from the heat of the stove. I should have put a bra on.

She laughs and shrugs. "I'll try, it's just a really nice chest!"

At this point I'm tempted to tell her to stop, that she's playing with fire. But the thing is, she isn't. I'm all thoughts, no action. Not with my marriage and best friend at stake. I'll just stand here, tortured by my own imagination and dirty mind.

"What?" she asks, and when I look at her she adds, "I can read you, Bex."

I take what I hope is an understated deep breath, then force a teasing tone into my voice. "You've upped your flirting with me lately, I'm starting to think Alec isn't paying enough attention to you."

"I haven't upped it!" she says, and she sounds legitimately defensive. It's possible that's true, that she's always been like this and I've only started noticing it recently. "I can pull it back if you need me to."

"You're fine," I say, flipping a pancake and then pouring another. What else can I say—'Please pull it back because apparently I have a crush on you and it's making things weird?'

"I just don't want to make things weird," she continues, apparently able to read my mind.

I force myself to laugh. "Darcy, it'll take a lot more than you flirting with me to make things weird. We're fine."

And we are. I refuse to let us be anything else, regardless of the fact that I really want to plaster the satin of her tank top to her nipples, lavish her with my tongue and teeth before I pull it up and off and finally get to taste her skin.

I clear my throat and present her with a plate of pancakes and warmed syrup. "Buen provecho," I say, and she again gives me that wistful smile.

***

Rafe joins us after Darcy and I are done eating and I'm mixing up another batch of pancakes. When he does, Darcy pulls on a sweatshirt that hides her nipples, the curve of her breasts, and that hint of cleavage I've been trying not to stare at, all morning. I choose not to read into it, not to assume that it means something that she wore a tiny top around me but not my husband. We were, after all, roommates for years, pajamas around each other is nothing new.

"Morning," Rafe says to Darcy, then grabs a handful of my shirt and hauls me against him. His lips press against mine and a hand grabs my ass and squeezes. I laugh into his mouth.

"No laughing, this kiss is very serious business," he growls and I nod, trying to figure out how to make him growl again, because I love when he does.

"Right, of course, the seriousest."

"Sounds like you're humoring me," he says, and his hand adjusts and slips into my shorts, right up against my skin because I'm not wearing any underwear. His fingers are rough and calloused, and I love the feel of them cupping my ass. I'm turned on by the fact that I can feel his erection against my stomach, turned on that we have an audience.

The idea of Darcy watching us and wishing she was Rafe is hot, of her squirming in those thin satin shorts as they get damp, of Alec finding them later and her telling him what she saw, of them having sex while they talk about some hot fantasy with all four of us in it.

I really need to stop.

"Darcy," I manage against his mouth, and it turns up in a grin.

"I'm Rafe, actually."

"Shut up." I pull back a bit to shove his shoulder, but his hand keeps my pelvis pressed firmly against him and he shifts intentionally against me, full of suppressed laughter.

"I mean we have an audience." I say.

Darcy grins broadly from her seat at the bar, and pipes up. "Oh, did you want me to buy tickets? Because I can, just tell me how much."

Rafe looks over at her and laughs, then looks back at me. He's imagining it, I can tell, her watching us and how much I'd like that. He wiggles his eyebrows.

"We'll discuss a price and let you know," he says.

I roll my eyes dramatically, shaking my head first at him, then at Darcy, as if I can't tell why I put up with them. Though really, I do because they're my two favorite people in the world.

I try to ignore how damp these shorts have gotten as my imagination runs away from me. Because I'm picturing myself on my back, Rafe standing between my legs and fucking me while Darcy sits on my face and I lick her senseless. I'm picturing how afterwards I want to grope her while she tastes herself on my mouth and sit on Rafe's face as he goes to town on me. How I want to fuck Rafe while Darcy watches from across the room, eyes hungry. Then they swap places and Darcy and I go down on each other, fuck each other with our fingers, while Rafe watches, wishing he could join in. I want them watching me like I'm hot and desirable and all they want is to *make* me come. But since they can't, they'll happily settle for *watching* me come and hope that they get a turn next.

"Pancake mix is done for whenever Alec's awake!" I say loudly. *Too* loudly. Because I need Alec to show up and distract Darcy, and honestly, to distract Rafe.

If you'd told me a week ago that Alec entering a room would make me *less* horny I wouldn't have believed you, but I cling to that hope, because I don't think I could physically stand the alternative. I'd just spontaneously combust, going up in flames from all the tension and desire in my body right now.

I turn to our bedroom. "I'm going to take a shower and get ready."

Chapter Eleven

I HATE COLD SHOWERS but there's no doubt that I need one right now, so I shuck off my clothes and hop in. It doesn't help, though, because the chill makes my nipples harden and my breasts feel tight, puckered. Goosebumps pop up all over my body and it makes my skin come alive, makes me aware of every square inch.

If I'm turned on enough that a cold shower isn't helping, I'm really fucked.

So I turn to plan B: slake my desire in the hopes that I can face Darcy today without imagining her naked, humping my bare thigh. One of my hands on her ass urging her on and another hand rolling a nipple between my thumb and forefinger. The delicate skin of her neck caught between my teeth, leaving a mark that she'll see every day for a week, until it finally fades to a yellow, and then disappears.

I turn the water to a more comfortable temperature and grab the handheld. Sitting down on the bench, I spread my legs, one foot on the floor and the other propped up next to me. Leaning against the cool tile walls, I close my eyes, taking a deep breath and directing the stream of water at the apex of my wide-open thighs.

My thumb is always a good place to start, strumming my clit like it's a guitar string. And the sensation from that only reinforces the imagery:

my body humming, vibrating with each stroke. I wish I had a free hand for my tits, to pluck and twist my nipples a little rough, just the way I like.

I'm out of hands though, so my imagination will have to do. After my conversation with Rafe last night, I can't help but think about the fact that maybe in a month or two I'll know what it's like to be with a woman, so the hands that I imagine touching me are smaller than his, softer. A little hesitant at first, trying to figure out what I like and what I don't, but I'm eager to show, and she picks up the specifics quickly.

Then she pushes my hand away from my clit, testing me there, trying me out. Discovering the secret to how I want to be touched. She's massaging my clit, and there's no doubt that it's swollen, it's swollen for *her*, it needs her touch. She's the only one that can give me the release I need, and she's up to the task, switching from her thumb to two fingers, rubbing me so fast.

"More," I gasp, and that's when she slides fingers into my pussy. Any hesitation she had a few minutes ago, when she was playing with my tits, is gone now. And fuck, I can't pretend like I'm imaging some nameless, faceless woman, because obviously I'm not.

Obviously, it's Darcy.

Darcy with her grin and her teasing laugh and that mouth I keep finding myself staring at this week. Darcy with that hair that would tickle my chest as she kissed her way down my body.

I'm supposed to be taking the edge off, exhausting my sexual energy so that I don't have any left when I'm around her, but all I'm doing is increasing it. Being around her is going to be even more unbearable, but right now I don't care because I'm imagining myself fucking her fingers, imagining those lips around my nipple, imagining that hair in my grasp.

And Darcy's sure now, confident, whispering in my ear. Telling me I'm gorgeous, telling me she's imagined this moment for so long, telling me she wants to see what I'm like when I come. The fingers on my clit and those inside me are moving so fast now, and I'm getting close, and I tell her so. Gasping and telling her that I can't wait to show her, that I'm right on the edge. That I need her so fucking much, that I'm so glad she's here, that I can't wait for her to see what she makes me do.

She tells me to come for her, and that's what pushes me over the edge. I clench around my fingers but pretend like they're Darcy's, like the showerhead pointed at my clit is her hand, like her mouth is wrapped around my tit, sucking hard, punishingly so.

Boneless, I let out a shaky sigh. The hand holding the shower head droops. I let go of it, breathing hard as I sit and let the other five showerheads pelt me with water.

I'm so fucked. I was supposed to slake my desire, not up it, but I accidentally did the latter and I have no idea how I'm supposed to go out there and face her today. Or how I'm supposed to face my husband.

It's not that he's the only person I've ever fantasized about. We're honest about the fact that sometimes we have crushes. They don't mean anything like we both love Rashida Jones and Kathryn Hahn and the barista at our local coffee joint. It crosses my mind that I should now ask him his favorite Chris.

But I've never fantasized about someone this close to me, to us. It feels dangerously close, to let a crush get this deep, especially when we're on vacation with her and her husband. It feels disloyal in a way that other crushes don't. Maybe because if we were both up for it, something could theoretically happen and that would just be asking for trouble. Hooking up with some random woman we meet at a sex club is one thing, hooking up with my best friend is another.

I'm sitting there, eyes still closed, trying to gather up the strength to stand up and soap myself down, to push what just happened out of my mind, to focus on Rafe and no one else for the remainder of the trip. And that's when I feel a mouth on my pussy.

Startled, I jolt and open my eyes to find Rafe there, kneeling on the floor. His tongue travels the distance from my clit to my opening, and then he pulls away.

"Watching you was so fucking hot. Were you imagining her?" he asks softly, and my face burns as I nod.

The smile he gives me is genuine as he reaches up to nudge the water a tad warmer. "This one's from me. Relax, mi vida. I've got you."

I shouldn't be surprised that he's not jealous, that he accepted my nod with a calm matter-of-factness, but I am. He knows that this side of me that I've been aware of for years has been getting louder and more insistent as I age. But knowing your wife is bi, and knowing she's masturbating while thinking about her best friend are two different things.

But maybe he's okay with it because he does it too? Maybe sometimes when he's in the shower it's not my hand he imagines on him, but Alec's?

And it turns out I'm okay with that. It brings me some peace about what I just did with an imaginary Darcy. I know he loves me, I know we love this life we've built together, and I know he's not going to abandon me to run off with Alec or anyone else. Who he thinks about when he's stroking himself off shouldn't worry me, because I trust him.

Which is why I tell myself not to *feel* guilty as he covers me with his mouth. I tangle my fingers in his hair, lay back against the shower wall and just give in.

I can move from fantasizing about Darcy to losing myself in Rafe's touch with surprising ease. They don't compete with each other, they complement each other. They fill different needs. The same way that sometimes I want to be bent over a table and fucked roughly as my underwear gets shoved to the side, while other times I want to make love on a bed, in missionary, then cuddle.

Rafe slips a finger inside me, then two. He goes for my G-spot, stroking it slowly and the moan I let out echoes off the walls. My own G-spot play doesn't do this, it's only Rafe, and he takes pride that it's only ever been him. His tongue on my clit, his finger caressing me from the inside, a hand squeezing my tit, water running down my body, the fact that I still haven't come down fully from my solo session—it all melds together to bring me up, quickly.

"That's it," he says quietly, his words vibrating against my pussy. "You're so fucking ready after imagining her that you're going to make my job easy."

I nod, then open my eyes to look at him, and the only way to describe the expression in his eyes is love. That's what he feels towards me right now, and the feeling is so mutual I can hardly stand it.

"I adore you," I tell him. "That's not even the right word, it's not strong enough. How I got this boy I had a crush on for years. This superhot, super athletic, super smart, super sweet, super everything boy, noticed me and married me and *fuck*!"

The last word is louder and followed by a groan, because his fingers against my G-spot have sped up, and now I've completely forgotten what I'm saying.

"Can I fuck you?" I say suddenly, urgently. That's what I want right now, I want him inside me, I want to taste myself on his mouth, I want his hands all over me. "Please, please let me fuck you."

He pulls away and shifts from kneeling to sitting, then pulls me over him. He's hard, which isn't a surprise, but I give him a couple of pumps with my hand, anyway. It's almost impossible for me to see his cock and not touch it. Then I position him at my opening and slide down on him, capturing his groan with my mouth.

One of his hands cups my ass, gripping my cheek to help me as I slide up and down his length. As the shower sprays water on us I move over him, burying my fingers in his hair, kissing him hard. Our height difference means we've never quite figured out standing sex in the shower, but I refused to give up on it completely, so at one point I convinced him to sit and let me straddle him. Since then, it's been a favorite, because the water running down our bodies means everything gets touched, every part of us gets attention. We also like doggie style, me on my hands and knees and him fucking me from behind, every thrust sending water flinging forward with the momentum, my tits swinging beneath me unless he decides to hold them in place. But today we're starting with straddling.

He keeps me from going too fast, a steady tempo that lets the energy in my body build slowly, keeps me from tipping over the edge too quickly. But it's not edging energy, it's not teasing, it's drawing the pleasure out, the same way he likes to savor a fancy meal or a glass of wine. When it's time to come, we'll come but there's no rush to get us there.

"Can I tell you how hot it would be to watch you?" he asks and my whole body reacts to those few words because maybe he's been thinking about it too.

Silently, I nod.

He lifts me off him and pushes me to my knees and then all fours and he settles behind me, entering me without warning. It's so fucking hot and my body welcomes the invasion.

"Was her mouth on your pussy or was it her fingers?" he asks, and I struggle to find my voice.

"Fingers," I manage, and he begins moving behind me, in and out, painfully slow.

"I can see that." His voice is rough, gravely with sex. "Maybe you'll be wearing some of those nylon shorts of yours that are so fucking sexy, and she'll slip her hands down them. I'll wonder if she's inside your underwear or not, but then your eyes will meet hers and I'll be able to tell she's inside them and just discovered how wet you are."

I swallow as his hand travels over my hip and between my legs, settling on my clit but not doing much there yet, just a bit of pressure.

"I can't quite tell what she's doing in there because it's hidden by your clothes. But every once in a while you catch your breath and sigh, so I know that she's starting to figure it out.

"And then I get lucky, because she strips you naked so she can see every part of you. Would you let her lay you out like that, not a stitch of clothing, legs spread, glistening for both her and me?"

I nod and his fingers press against my clit then disappear, causing me to buck and chase the sensation. But he's too quick and I miss him.

"Then I see what she's doing and it's not quite right. Don't get me wrong, It's a valiant effort. But you've got a way that you like to be touched and she doesn't know that yet, so you cover her hand with yours and show her."

Yet. He said yet. In this fantasy of his, which I'm not quite sure whether it's improv or something he's pictured before, there's a yet. That means there might be a fantasy next time, an *again*.

"Oh, fuck," he continues. "You just spasmed around my cock so I know you like that, but you've always liked introducing people to your clit and your pussy, giving them an orientation. I remember when you did that for me, in my apartment back in college, when you took my hand and slid it into your underwear and showed me this"—he strokes my clit up and down with his thumb—"and this"—he makes a slow torturous circle—"and this." My clit gets the lightest little pinch, because back in college that's all I was willing to try, so desperate to be a good girl that any desire that wasn't vanilla got completely ignored. Not that we're Rocky Road at this point, but at the very least we occasionally shake some sprinkles on.

"You were so shy that night, you weren't sure if I'd like being shown, but honestly that's the thing that made me fall in love with you, even though I didn't want to use that word yet. Your willingness to grab the bull by the horns, to show me what you wanted, to demand pleasure."

He's told me before, but today the words feel heavier, more significant.

"But with Darcy, with Darcy you don't have to be shy. You can be assertive, show her exactly what you want and need to come, because both she and I want you to come.

"You're so fucking hot when you come, Rebecca, I'm not sure if you realize just how much. I wish we hadn't deleted the tape we made that one time. Because I'd watch it every time I needed to come and you weren't around, I love to see your whole body flush. To see your nipples get hard because they're a giveaway of how turned on you are. If I'm not inside you, I can tell that you're horny and want to fuck because they pop out. Anyone who's been paying attention knows that about you. The way your mouth parts and your breathing gets faster.

"And if she's fingering you, Darcy would get to see all that close up, would get to feel your chest rising and falling with each breath, would get her fingers slick with the feel of you. And I'd be equal parts so goddamn jealous of her because she gets you for a few minutes and so goddamn turned on to see you fucking her hand like you're about to lose control."

Rafe is the one that's starting to lose control though. I know because we've been together for so long, because other than my own he's the only orgasm that I've experienced in over a decade and a half.

His fingers grip my hips so hard I might have indentations for a week, fucking me hard and fast from behind. I can even feel his balls slapping me with every thrust.

"And once you've taught her how to get you off, where to touch you and how to touch you and the specific moves that are going to make you come, you pull your hand away and let her do it herself.

"I can see you tracing her lips with the hand that's dripping with your ambrosia, and her capturing those fingers in her mouth and sucking them clean. Then because you're so fucking obsessed with how you taste—and who can blame you, I'm obsessed with it too—you pull her in for a kiss because you want to taste yourself on her."

Then he stops talking, hands gripping me. My clit is left all alone, so I reach down for it, stroking and circling until I'm gasping and he's gasping. I know we're both close, both of us getting off on this idea that I'm with someone other than him and it feels both so fucking wrong yet so fucking right. I'm tired of things feeling wrong because I've been told they're supposed to feel wrong, so I push that thought away and embrace the rightness of it. Of imagining getting off with Darcy as Rafe watches.

"Fuck, Bex," he gasps.

I'm right on the edge too, my hand working furiously. The water cascading down my back and along my legs, my hair dripping, him slamming into me. It's both too much and not enough.

"I'm gonna..." I whisper.

"Do it," he replies.

And I do.

Afterwards he pulls me into his lap, still sitting on the floor of the shower as the water streams on us. I'm probably dripping the evidence of what we've just done onto his leg, but he doesn't seem to mind.

"You think this is what she meant when she kept telling us to break the shower in?" I joke, and he brushes some sopping hair out of my face.

"I'm starting to wonder, to be honest."

I roll my eyes, but he doesn't join in.

"You're not the only one staring, mi vida. I think this attraction goes both ways."

"Shut up," I say, scrambling to get to my feet. He releases me immediately, but doesn't stand up. "That's not funny."

"It's not a joke," he says simply, carefully.

"Well then what do we do?" I'm trying not to panic, because fantasizing about being with my best friend and the reality that it might be possible are two very different things.

"Only what you feel comfortable with," is his answer, because he's Rafe and he's too good and I don't deserve him.

"I mean hooking up with someone random and hooking up with Darcy are two totally different things. Darcy isn't who we were talking about last night."

"She wasn't?" he asks, and my knees almost give out under me because—

"Wait, you were?"

"You weren't?"

I think the honest answer is that I wasn't. It never actually crossed my mind that Darcy was a real possibility. But now that it has, I'm not sure how to exorcize the idea.

I redirect. "Were you talking about Alec?"

The chuckle he gives is half-hearted, self-deprecating, and he shakes his head. "I think I'm going to need a lot more time to get used to the idea of... not being straight."

"Of being bi or pan or queer?" I prompt.

His Adam's apple bobs in a swallow. "Of being queer," he supplies, and then glances at me as if he wants to make sure I'm okay with the fact that he's said it, picked that word.

I give his hand a squeeze and he continues. "I need to fully adjust to being queer before I start hooking up with dudes," he says.

I nod, though I'm not entirely sure that's true. But it's not my place to say so instead I settle back in his lap, resting my forehead against his cheek.

"You don't have to be okay with me doing it, either. You can hook up with Darcy or some other woman, that doesn't mean you have to give me your okay. This doesn't have to be a tit for tat situation," he says.

I believe that he means it because the opposite would be true as well—I wouldn't feel owed a hookup if he did. But I also wonder if he's saying that as an excuse not to. It's a lot easier to ignore your own feelings if you're telling yourself your wife wouldn't like it anyway.

"And you can," he adds. "If the opportunity comes up and you want to."

"Fuck, I don't know," I say honestly. "I was thinking we'd revisit it in a month, not a day."

He presses a kiss to my forehead and doesn't say anything else, so we just sit there in silence, letting the water run over us.

"Oh!" I suddenly remember something that had struck me earlier. "Important question."

He pulls away to look at me, and I grin.

"Now that I know you're queer. Which Chris?"

Rafe laughs then presses a kiss to my mouth. "There's only one answer to that," he says, breaking out his most irresistible grin.

At the same time we both answer, "Evans."

Chapter Twelve

THE PLAN TODAY IS to skip the beach this morning and go for a walk instead. There are a handful of trails, and we visit the nature center to learn about all the wildlife to look for before we head out.

Alec is an amateur photographer. He refuses to call himself even that, but his pictures are fucking amazing. Whenever we get together he's constantly sending us pictures of our kids, of us playing with them, of our families laughing. I'll never need to pay a professional photographer again because his stuff is that good. And today he's brought his camera along, saying he wants to work on his nature photography skills.

But soon I notice that he's sneaking more pictures of Darcy than of the trees and birds. I'm not sure she's aware—they're mostly pictures of her in profile, reading something, looking for something, observing something.

He catches me watching him and I grin, nodding to the viewer. "Can I see?"

Alec hands the camera over to me and I scroll through the pictures. Honestly, Darcy is a snack and a half. I tell him that, hoping it sounds teasing and not like someone with a crush.

He grins. "She really is. I'm lucky that I got her."

"You are," I agree, as I continue to scroll through but then catch my breath because there's a picture of Rafe and it's just as gorgeous. He's gripping a railing, looking forward—probably trying to identify one of the birds from the pamphlet we got—and you can see the definition of his forearm muscles, flexed under the tattoos on his right arm. His face is deep in concentration, handsome as ever, hair tucked in a baseball cap that shadows him and makes him look mysterious. The back of his shirt has ridden up just a tiny bit, a strip of skin exposed.

"You are, too," Alec says quietly.

When I glance at him he looks away, as if he doesn't want me to see whatever's in his eyes.

"I am," I agree, and turn back to the camera, wondering if I'm assigning meaning where there isn't any.

There aren't any pictures of me on his roll—just a ton of Darcy and a smattering of Rafe. And honestly, it's exactly what I want to see, two of my favorite people in the world through Alec's eyes.

It strikes me that Alec and I may have similar tastes.

"Thanks for letting me look," I say, handing back the camera. "They're all amazing, I want copies of, like, all of them."

"What are you going to do with a few dozen pictures of my wife?" he asks, and his voice is teasing but I can't help it, my face heats anyway. I have the worst poker face known to man.

"What are you going to do with a handful of pictures of my husband?" I ask back, eyebrows quirked. I know Alec well enough to recognize his laughter is self-conscious.

"Touché," he says, and I try to figure out if we just secretly admitted something to each other.

Suddenly I wonder if he's fucked Darcy while telling her how much he wants to see her fingers buried in my pussy. It takes all my self-control not to run to the ocean at the end of this boardwalk and fling myself in, to cool off. My nipples are puckering and wetness is pooling between my legs and I don't care who I fuck but I really want to fuck someone. Like, right now.

Then I feel arms around my waist and look up. It's Rafe, pressing a kiss to my temple. I turn to face him, wrapping my arms around his neck and brush my lips against his. But just briefly because if I get started, I'll end up humping him in public. And no one wants to see that.

"You look like you're thinking things," he says. He sounds concerned, so I laugh and shake my head, moving my mouth right next to his ear.

"Things that aren't safe for public," I whisper. He chuckles, the low sound shooting right through me.

His mouth finds mine and he gives me a real kiss, which is dangerous with how turned on I am. His hand wanders lower, grabbing my ass, and that's when I hear the click of the camera.

We pull away, glancing at Alec, who's grinning at us. "Sorry," he says, though he sounds like he doesn't mean it. "It was just too good a picture not to take."

Rafe laughs and spins me towards him, trapping my lower body between his pelvis and the wooden railing.

"You want a great picture of me kissing my wife? I'll give you one," he says, but he's looking at me, question in his eyes: *You up for a little PDA?*

I nod, because apparently I've been bitten by the exhibitionism bug, and his grin widens as he leans in to kiss me.

It's a passionate kiss, intense, and I groan into his mouth. Through his exercise shorts I feel him getting hard. One of his hands coasts over my hip, ass, upper thigh and then pulls my leg up and around him. As my legs spread as he settles against me, just perfect. The thin layers of clothing means that I can feel all of him against my clit, against my opening, and it's near impossible not to move against him. But maybe we should draw the line at dry humping in public.

The click of the camera is faint and easy to ignore as his other hand slides up my stomach, cupping my breast. Then his thumb rubs against my nipple, which pebbles. And fuck it, I guess we're dry humping in public. I need to do *something* to lessen this string of tension that he's building in me.

Rafe's hand slides down again, and this time slips under my shirt then pauses. I know this move: he's asking if it's okay, so I give the universal *yes do whatever you want to me, I don't care because I'm horny as fuck* sign. At least, I hope that's the message he gets when I tighten one hand in his hair and slip the other hand down, tucking it under the hem of his shirt.

If Darcy and Alec are to the left of us they have a view of my shirt pulled up over my tit and Rafe playing with me over my bra. If they're on the other side they see my leg hiked up around his waist as we grind, his hand hidden my shorts so his fingers can tease my skin right at the line of my panties. If they're behind Rafe they see a bare leg wrapped around his back while my hand pulls up his shirt to trace his skin.

I hope they're half as turned on *watching* us as I am *being* us, and going by the way I can hear the camera clicking, it's very possible.

But then Darcy's whisper breaks through my hormone-addled mind. "Someone's coming."

We pull apart almost immediately, both of us pulling our shirts down and then looking over the other. I readjust Rafe's baseball hat and he smooths my shorts down over my leg.

But fuck, his lips are swollen, his eyes are glazed, and he looks like he sometimes does post-fuck. It's the kind of look that makes me want to pounce on him again, telling him I need more of his dick, to which he always laughs, pretending like it's a chore to fuck my pussy or my mouth again.

We finally tear our eyes away from each other.

"Sorry," he says at the same time as I say, "Guess we got a little carried away."

"Never be sorry for that," Darcy says, though there's a tension, a low quality in her voice, as if she's forcing the words past something.

"Hot as fuck," Alec agrees, and that's when I notice the outline of his bulge through his sweatpants is a little more obvious.

Is it weird to be proud that I made my best friend's husband half-hard? Probably, but I am anyway. Especially since I'm pretty sure Rafe has more to do with his half-chub than I do.

The group that Darcy heard walks by us and we do our best not to look like we're more turned on than anyone should be in public. God, I really need to be fucked again.

This trip is making me insatiable.

"We should probably head home anyway," Rafe says quietly, and we nod.

"I'll drive," Alec says. "I kind of just went overboard with the pictures, so you guys should look and decide if there's any you'd rather I delete."

"And which ones you want to print out," Darcy adds, and there's a twinkle in her eye like somewhere in their house there are a bunch of pictures printed out of her. My pussy clenches at the thought.

"Right," Rafe says. He looks at me as he wiggles his eyebrows and takes my hand. "Let's get back then."

The pictures are so fucking sexy and remind me that *I* can be so fucking sexy. With Rafe obviously, but on my own, too. There's one picture where his face is hidden, buried in my neck, and my head is thrown back, stomach and chest exposed, and a hint of lace visible under his hand that's palming my breast.

"Fuck," I say, under my breath. It looks like an actual piece of art, intimate and gorgeous, and you can practically *see* the sex oozing off me.

"What?" Rafe asks, and I blush because it feels weird to say, but it's also definitely true.

"I'm really hot sometimes," I whisper.

He grips my chin, turning my face towards his. "*Always*, mi vida."

He kisses me and it's soft. It isn't sex, it's love, and I feel it wrapping around me like a cozy comfortable blanket.

"What do we do if they're getting it on in the back seat?" Darcy stage-whispers and Rafe and I pull away, laughing.

"You made them self-conscious," Alec whispers back. "I was hoping for a show."

It's not the first time someone's made a joke like that this week, and I wonder if that's something they've talked about. If while they heard us fucking through the walls on our second night here they wanted to see us, not just hear us. If in their mind's eye they saw Rafe slamming into me from behind or my tits bouncing as I rode him, or if they were content just listening.

I'm trying not to label or judge these thoughts and images I'm having of Darcy, or of Darcy and Alec, or of Rafe and Alec. None of the labels would be good or have positive connotations, and I firmly believe that fantasies are okay so long as they don't go past that. I'm also starting to wonder if going past it is okay so long as everyone is enthusiastically on board.

But nothing's going to happen—not this week, not with them. This is setting Rafe and I up for some exploration when we get home, and that's all.

This is real life, where nothing more than that actually happens. Especially not to people like me.

Chapter Thirteen

FOR LUNCH WE RIDE our bikes to a food truck park on the island. After ordering from different places for the main meal, we meet up at the ice cream truck for dessert. I'm halfway through my ice cream sandwich when I notice how quickly it's melting, making a bit of a mess on my fingers. It's not just mine, either—a trail of ice cream dribbles down Darcy's cone, then her arm, and I find myself staring as she chases it with her tongue. She catches the dribble when it's halfway down her wrist and licks her way up to the crease between her pointer finger and thumb, then envelops the delicate flap of skin there in her mouth.

I'm jealous. I want her tongue working on me like that, I want her to suck my skin with that kind of enthusiasm. I lick my lips as I watch her, and then she glances up and catches me staring.

There's heat in her stare and I should look away but I can't, and she doesn't either. Instead, our eyes stay trained on each other while her tongue licks her skin clean and then moves on to her cone and *fuck*. It's too much. The idea that Rafe might be right, that the attraction isn't one-sided, resurfaces. It seems almost certain now.

I'm about to do something stupid, say something stupid, tip my hand, when a fat raindrop hits my nose.

Rafe grabs my hand and pulls me under the awning of one of the food trucks, wrapping his arms around me so that I'm as covered and out of the rain as possible.

His voice is quiet in my ear. "Do you want me to talk you into it or out of it?"

I pull away to look at him, and his expression is matter-of-fact. Curious, but calm.

"I don't know," I say, which feels like an admission in and of itself. Because really, I'm supposed to know whether or not I want to kiss someone other than my husband. Whether I want to strip my best friend naked and have her writhing beneath me. Whether I want someone new to make me come.

"I want you to think about it. And if you decide yes, know that I fully support you. If you decide no, I'll happily volunteer to let you take all your energy out on me." He tucks a strand of hair behind my ear adding, "And no matter what you decide, I'll love you more than life itself."

I study him for a beat, then kiss him, because that's the only acceptable response to a statement so kind and loving and thoughtful.

The owner of the food truck interrupts us, leaning out the order window.

"We're going to close up. Rain's going to continue for another hour or two."

The four of us look at each other, because we're obviously not going to huddle under cover for that long.

"I can ride back and go get the car," Alec offers.

I shake my head. "It's not raining that hard. Why don't we all just ride back together."

So we do, and when we get home we're soaked to the bone, wet clothes clinging to our bodies.

I can see Alec's pecs and Rafe's back muscles flex under his. And *fuck*, Darcy's white shirt is now essentially see-through. I can see the lace edges of her bra. I can make out the tops of her breasts where they slope down gently. I can even almost feel the weight of her in my hands, and how she'd fit so perfectly into my palm.

I saw her in a bra the first day after padiddle, and I've seen plenty of cleavage over the past few days thanks to her swimsuits. I saw hard nipples under a silk tank top this morning, but this, *this* is what almost breaks my resolve.

"We should change into dry clothes," Alec says, and once again I'm saved from doing something stupid.

"Into or out of?" Rafe asks again when we're alone in our bathroom and I shrug because what I *want to do* and what I *should do* are more at war than I ever remember them being.

He motions for me to raise my arms. Carefully he removes my wet clothes, and I'm almost naked when we hear a voice at our bedroom door.

"Suits for the hot tub when the rain ends?" Alec calls.

Rafe agrees and that's when I realize Darcy hasn't said a word since I eye-fucked her as she ate ice cream.

I reach for one of my suits, but Rafe offers me the other one instead.

Neither of the suits I brought are tiny by any stretch of the imagination—I'm pushing 40, after all—but this one is definitely smaller. The bottoms are a little cheekier, the top has an underwire that supports me better and makes my tits look great. Rafe's favorite part is untying the suit with his teeth.

I glance at him, not sure how to ask the question that's forming in my mind.

He watches me carefully. "If you want."

"This is so weird," I admit. But I pull on the swimsuit because we both know I want to. He wouldn't be so encouraging if I didn't.

Still, I shrug on a cover-up.

The rain is still steady, so instead of the hot tub we watch another *Avengers* movie. Darcy is being uncharacteristically quiet, and I try not to let it distract me as I glance at her on the loveseat with Alec. She's superhot in both of the suits she brought, but I'll admit that the one she's wearing right now is my favorite of the two. Alec's hand is over her shoulder but drooping down, lightly tracing along the deep 'V' neckline.

I try not to wish his hand was mine, traversing the slope of her breast, and instead focus back on the movie.

"Leftovers for dinner?" Rafe asks, after the movie's over as we stretch, standing up.

"Dibs on the pizza," Darcy and I say in unison, and then crack smiles, but even that seems weighted, not as light and playful as usual.

"Y'all can split it," Rafe promises and Alec opens a bottle of wine to pour everyone a glass.

There's a silent conversation between him and Darcy when he hands over her glass. I try to ignore her nervous, questioning smile. Try not to read into the way he raises his eyebrows at her and then winks. He dips his head closer to hers and whispers something in her ear, and I see her quietly ask *Oh?* After his whispered response she laughs and shakes her head, giving his shoulder a light shove.

Whatever he said seems to loosen her up, though. That and the glass of wine she drinks deeply from.

I do the same.

Halfway through the second movie the wine has lessened some of the tension for all of us, though I'm still studiously avoiding eye contact with Darcy. Alec stands up and starts rummaging through the hall closet where we'd noticed a bunch of board games earlier in the week. Then we hear a victorious, "Ah-ha!"

"You okay babe?" Darcy asks, pausing the movie as he reappears with a white box in his hands.

"I have our next activity," he says, and then turns it around to show us. Twister.

"Um, no," Darcy says, laughing.

Rafe grins and nods. "Um, yes," he says, standing up and holding his hand out for me, pulling me up.

"I haven't played drunk Twister in..." I search my memory, trying to remember. "Years," is where I settle.

"No time like the present," Rafe says. He tugs on my cover-up. "Take it off, this is going to get all tangled up."

"I'm good," I say, afraid I'd feel naked without it, even though neither of the guys are wearing shirts and Darcy is wearing just her suit as well.

"Suit yourself," Darcy says, and I can't tell if the tone I'm sensing from her is disappointment or relief.

The game starts simple enough, but soon Alec starts encroaching on Darcy's territory and she's got to figure out how to stretch across him when she spins left foot red.

Rafe decides to be a troublemaker as well, and when he needs to move his right hand, instead of just sliding it from yellow to green, he decides to snake it between my body and my cover-up.

"The hell?" I ask laughingly.

He wiggles his eyebrows. "Told you it was going to get tangled."

"You're being sabotaged," Darcy says. Even though she's barely talked to me all evening, her eyes are twinkling and teasing. I realize I'd just imagined that there was tension between us.

"I think I am."

When I next have the opportunity to move a hand, I reach up to slip the cover-up over my head, freeing myself before putting my hand back down.

Rafe laughs and nibbles at the skin of my side. When I shift to shake my ass in his face, his mouth opens wide and he bites my exposed cheek.

No wonder he wanted me to wear the cheeky bottoms.

Alec's move is next. It puts him within kissing distance of Darcy, so they do, and then a few turns later Rafe's crotch ends up near Alec's face.

I see Rafe's Adam's apple bob in a nervous swallow, but Alec doesn't seem to notice or be fazed, probably because he's staring at Darcy's chest where one of her tits looks like it's about to break free of her swimsuit.

I give Rafe a *look* and he gives me a tight smile as Darcy moves, stretching her arm a little further, even more of her cleavage slipping past her swimsuit neckline.

I'm trying to figure out if what I'm seeing is the edge of her areola or just a shadow when I realize I'm staring and glance away just in time to see Alec's spin, which basically lines up his crotch with Rafe's ass. I can't tell if there's a flicker of panic in Alec's eyes or if I just imagined it, but Rafe's eyes close and don't open. I know his 'struggling to not get hard' expression when I see it. Then his next move makes him back up a step and his ass presses fully into Alec's crotch.

I think we all know that the fall that follows almost immediately is fake, but no one calls him on it.

Then it switches to the three of us, and apparently there's a strategy to Twister because Alec corrals Darcy and I into a corner and next thing I know every move has a different part of my body right up against hers. My arm presses against her chest, or our bare legs tangle up, or my mouth is inches from her shoulder.

"Seriously?" I ask Rafe, who took over spinning and calling when he went out, because the most recent move will put my face right up against her tits—including the one that at this point is only still in her swimsuit by magic.

Rafe tosses back a sarcastic, "No, I'm making it up."

My head swivels around to look at him and the guilty expression is only on his face a millisecond before he wipes it away and shrugs. "Right hand blue," he repeats.

So I move, sighing as I do. I see goosebumps appear along the deep 'V' of Darcy's suit like she can feel my breath on her. A shadow of a nipple pops up as well, and I'm really glad that no one's near my crotch because I'm definitely damp between my legs.

There's a thumping sound and when I look over Alec is on the floor, though I have no idea why because it wasn't his turn, nor was he contorted in a particularly complicated position.

"I'll spin," he says, popping to his feet, and he and Darcy exchange a look I refuse to interpret. My mind briefly descends to a place where our husbands are scheming to have us hook up, but that would be beyond bizarre.

Then again, the next move Alec calls out gives her the option to straddle my leg. She hesitates for a moment because now that it's just the two of us she could just pick another yellow dot. But I can almost hear her think *fuck it* and then her legs are wrapped around mine.

Now it's my turn, and the move Rafe calls gives me the option of sliding under her, our breasts pressed against each other, or I can retreat.

I don't retreat.

Three more moves, each one giving us the option to get a little more tangled up, or move away, and we always choose the former. The room is starting to feel warm and I'm a little lightheaded. Darcy's skin is smooth and soft and butterflies take over my stomach.

One more call, it's Darcy's turn to move, and I'm pretty sure it's accidental but her foot slips and she collapses, tumbling down. Since I'm under her, I end up pinned between her and the mat.

"Hi," Darcy says, our fronts pressed together, legs tangled, and her smooth skin gliding against mine.

"Hi yourself," I say, my voice thick with forced lightness.

She crosses her arms on my chest and rests her chin on them, like she's settling in, and I can't help but laugh.

"Comfortable?" I ask.

She nods, a ghost of a smile on her face. "You?"

I nod.

"Am I squishing you?"

I shake my head.

"Do you want me to move?"

No! my body screams. *I want you closer!*

But instead of saying that, I just shrug.

My heart is pounding because her face is less than a foot away and it would be so easy to move my head just a bit and claim her mouth with mine. She might be thinking the same thing, because her eyes are focused on my lips. When I lick them, she groans.

"Bex," she says.

If she had anything else on her mind, she doesn't share it and the room is quiet again.

Do it! my hormone-addled brain yells.

Best friend! the logical side yells back.

Obviously wants it! the horny side insists.

Okay but—the logical side starts.

I tell it to shut up and close the inches between us, pressing my mouth to hers.

Chapter Fourteen

It's been years since I've had a first kiss with anyone. Seventeen, actually. I'd forgotten so many things about them. The butterflies and excitement I remember, but not the paralyzing fear that they might not kiss you back. And for the half-second when her lips are still against mine, that fear floods my body, ice cold.

But then her mouth softens, and she kisses me back. She slides off me and settles next to me, cradling my head with her hand. Her tongue traces my upper lip and I eagerly open up for her, turning my head to better fit our mouths together, brushing my tongue against hers.

It's Darcy. It's everything. I'm kissing my best friend and it's everything.

Then, from the general direction of the couch, I hear someone clear their throat. We separate immediately, scrambling to our knees because at the exact same moment we remember we're married and our husbands are *right there*.

"Shit, Alec, I'm sorry," I say, because I just kissed his wife and I'm so fucking embarrassed and worried. Rafe and I have talked about it, but there are two other people involved here and I should have asked. There's a way to be super smooth, to do a confident 'I really want to kiss you' thing, but instead I just attacked her with my mouth. This is one of those times it's *not* better to ask for forgiveness than permission.

"I'm sorry," I say to Darcy as well, feeling my face heat up because even if she kissed me back, I should have checked first.

"I've never... I should have..." I bury my face in my hands. "Oh My God, I thought college was full of the most awkward hookups ever and now I go and do this. And just because Rafe is cool with it doesn't mean you and Alec are and *fuck*."

I've just torpedoed my friendship with Darcy. This can't get any more humiliating.

"What do you mean Rafael's cool with it?" Darcy asks, her voice whisper quiet.

I take back what I said about it not being able to get more humiliating. I glance at Rafe, not sure how to explain that we've discussed the fact I'm hot for Darcy and he's cool with us hooking up.

He clears his throat. "We discussed it."

"Discussed what, exactly?" Alec asks.

"That if Bex wants to..."—he pauses, and I can tell that he's trying to figure out the right words. I'm beyond thankful he's taken the lead—"...explore other parts of her sexuality with a woman, I'm comfortable with it."

I look down at my hands, because I don't want to meet anyone's gaze. I feel exposed, naked, but not in the sexy way, in the 'everyone's pointing and laughing' way. The room is silent as I study my cuticles. After what feels like forever I glance up and see Alec and Darcy having a conversation with their eyes. Alec gives a nod, and then Darcy turns to me.

"Can I kiss you?"

I swear to God my heart stutters.

I glance at Rafe, who's got a little smile, and he nods so I do, too. Darcy wraps her hand around the back of my neck and pulls me to her.

Kisses me again.

This time it's slower. Gentler. We don't have to rush, there isn't the urgency of only getting one moment together. We can take time and enjoy ourselves, tongues brushing against each other's, her fingers skimming the skin of my neck, mine skimming down her sides, resting on the angles of her hips. She's softer than Rafe. Her hips give in to lush thighs and a plush stomach and a handful of ass.

God, I want to grab her tits. I want to know what they're like. I want her skin under my lips, I want my tongue to trace her areola and my breath to bring her nipples to a hard peak that I then suck into my mouth.

But this is just a make out. First base, that's all.

She pulls away, breathless.

"Bedroom?"

Fuck yes.

I nod, then glance at Rafe who also nods. Alec does too, so she stands up and takes my hand, pulling me to my feet. Without a word, the four of us go to Alec and Darcy's room. The guys settle on opposite sides while Darcy and I just glance at the bed, then at each other.

She bursts into a laugh. "This is so weird."

It is. "But good, right?" I check in, and she nods and her eyes go to my mouth and she licks her lips so I just lean forward and kiss her. Because that's all I want to do right now.

Well, maybe not *all* I want to do.

"Safe word?" she asks a little breathlessly when we finally pull apart. "So that if it goes too far or becomes too much we can tap out?"

I nod, wondering what would be 'too much' for me. The fact that I don't know the answer seems telling. Or maybe it's that I know it, but don't want to admit it.

"Suggestions?"

She glances at Alec. "When we have one, we use colors. Yellow, maybe?"

I swallow. "Yeah."

We're doing this.

She crawls onto the bed and takes my hand, tugging me towards her. "Then c'mere."

A moment later we're laying on the bed, hands wandering. I grasp her breast and discover it's soft and lovely, the perfect handful. She seems to be enjoying exploring my body as much as I am hers. Hands coasting over my suit, then my skin, then my suit again. Covering my bikini top with her hands as her mouth attaches itself to my neck. Teeth grazing my collarbone as she pinches the nipples that have pebbled under her touch.

"Fuck, Darcy," I mutter, and she laughs.

I love her laugh, but I want more. I want to know what it's like to make her arch against me, to be the one that causes those sounds I've heard through the wall this week.

That she made for her husband.

It's been seventeen years since I kissed anyone other than Rafe. Is it super fucked up that I'm doing this? A week ago, Darcy was my best friend but now, what does this make us?

I glance at Rafe, and he's looking back at me, eyes as hungry as I've ever seen them. There's a movement, and that's when I notice he's rubbing himself through his pants. Oh God, watching us has him super turned on. If this is fucked up, then at least we both are.

"You okay?" she asks.

I turn to look at Darcy, who's pulled back and is watching me, concerned.

"Yeah."

She raises her eyebrows, calling me on my bluff. She's the one person in the world who knows me as well as Rafe does.

"You can safe out, you know."

The words are said without any malice, very matter of fact, and her eyes watch me carefully as she tucks a strand of hair behind my ear.

Leaning forward, I kiss her. "I don't want to."

It's all the encouragement she needs, and she kisses me back, hard, slipping her tongue between my lips. I taste the wine she had tonight, but that was hours ago. By now we're basically sober.

We're doing this sober.

Her hands coast down my body, and the tips of her fingers slip under the waistline of my bottoms. Not far, probably not even past the first knuckle, but I feel my body clench in anticipation. Is she going to? Do I want this?

The answers are easy: *fuck I hope so*, and *fuck yes*.

Then she says into my ear, "What were our school colors?"

I pull back, confused at the question. Why is she asking me this?

"Blue and..." I start, then freeze. Yellow. She's checking to see if I want to safe out.

Her fingers slip down another inch.

"And?" she prompts.

My heart's beating so loudly in my chest I swear she can hear it. I shift, spreading my legs a little bit. Propping one knee up to give her all the access she needs. Another glance at Rafe, who licks his lips and gives the tiniest of nods, and all the air leaves my body for a moment.

"Pretty sure it was just blue."

Darcy laughs, and a moment later her hand has finished its journey, has discovered how embarrassingly wet I am.

"Fuck, Bex," she says, almost sounding awed, and my pussy gives a small spasm as my best friend's hand cups me.

At first, she takes her time, exploring me slowly, gently. I pull her closer for a kiss, and every time I groan into her mouth, she laughs into mine.

"I was so obsessed when I heard you the other night," she admits. "I love that now you're making noises for me."

I open my eyes and look at her, my best friend who's playing with my pussy, who's... well, I'm not sure if what she's doing is *technically* fingering, but God I want her inside me, so I slip a hand down to join hers, sliding her down to my opening.

Our eyes lock as her finger circles my entrance, and when she finally slides in my groan is the most desperate one yet. I don't feel self-conscious, even though I know Alec and Rafe are watching me, because it's so fucking good. I feel sexy and desirable, and it turns out I love being watched. I spread my legs a little more, moving against her hand as a second finger joins the first, then a third, and then Darcy's fucking me with her fingers as I ride her hand.

"How do I make you come?" she asks, and I put my thumb to work, rubbing my clit the way I love, then guiding her through the movement.

I get close, close, close to my peak, then put my hand over hers to stop for a moment, to dip away from climax.

Then I start back up again.

Darcy's eyes flash with heat. "Ohhhhh, edging? Bring you close and then pull back? Fuck, never imagined this side of you."

Then her head dips close to mine, and she whispers so that only I can hear, "And I imagined more often than I'd like to admit."

The confession takes my breath away, and I look up at her and she smiles. "You think I've never noticed you like that? God, Bex, you're *so* my type. You're just so fun and funny and gorgeous and confident. And now I'm figuring out this one last part of you that I didn't know, and I want you to come apart under my hands. I want to see in person what you tortured me with through the walls these past few days, I want to hear it without anything muffling it. Are you going to come for me?"

By now I'm not really guiding her because she's figured it out. She keeps bringing me to the edge and then backing off, and holy crap when I come it's going to be intense.

I glance at Rafe, who at this point has gone all out, dick in hand, as he strokes himself, watching us, watching *me* more intently than ever before. A quick glance at Alec and I see his gorgeous face is pained, like he feels bad about how turned on he is by this.

But I'm turned on too, knowing I'm being watched, knowing Rafe is masturbating because I'm being fingered by a woman and he thinks it's hot. There's a heady kind of power in knowing you're the reason someone had to pull their dick out of their pants, knowing they want to fuck you but someone else gets to right now.

Darcy gives my clit a pinch and I jolt, looking at her.

"I want your eyes here when you come," she says, then leans forward to give me a kiss. "Rafael gets you every night, but tonight I want you to know I'm the one doing this."

I nod and her hand increases its pace just a tad. Either I'm an awesome teacher or she's a quick study, because each time she gets me a little bit closer, and when she backs off the relief isn't quite enough for me to catch my breath. The coil in my body tightens and I start riding her hand intensely, not really caring what it might look like, that I'm being watched, just wanting the relief. She pulls back again and I whimper and whine.

"Stop it!" I demand, and she just laughs and shakes her head.

"Do you know how hot you look right now? Your cheeks are flushed and your whole lower half is involved in getting my hand as far up in you as possible. I can barely even tell where your clit is, that's how wet you are for me, and your whole body is glistening with this layer of sweat that's so fucking sexy because you worked it up with me. I don't know what I want more, to see what you're like when you come, or to just do this forever."

"Please make me come," I beg, even though the only other person I've begged in bed is Rafe. Pleading for an orgasm is the sort of thing I can only do with someone I trust beyond measure, and that's Rafe. But here I am, in bed with my best friend, and I'm already begging, after all of thirty minutes.

"Please," I repeat, "I need to come so bad."

"Are you going to come on my fingers?" she asks, and I nod, whimpering.

"Are you going to squeeze my fingers when you do, will I feel you spasm around them? Hey Rafael," she says, looking at my husband. "What's she like when she comes?"

I hear his voice from across the room, gravelly and rough, and my pussy clenches again. "You think she's wet now, just wait."

There's a pause where he clears his throat, then asks, "How many fingers do you have in there right now?"

"Switching back and forth between two and three."

"Fuck." I hear his head drop back against the wall, hear him take a shaky breath. "Stick with three, you'll be able to feel her squeeze around you better. You find her G-spot yet?"

"Um..."

"Stroke up with your fingers," he tells her.

Darcy's eyebrows wrinkle in concentration, and then she presses on it. I jolt against her, letting out a cry loud enough that it's possible the neighbors heard it.

I clasp my hands over my mouth.

"Yep, that's it," Rafe says, and I don't know if I've ever heard him chuckle so goddamn seductively. "Play with her clit, and as soon as she starts coming, rub her G-spot too. It's the best thing ever. She's so fucking gorgeous when she comes like that."

I'm probably supposed to feel weirded out that my husband is telling my best friend all my sexual secrets, but by now we're way past weird. We're in a space where two of the people I care about most in the world are focused on my pleasure. And I want to come for them, show Rafe that he's a good teacher, show Darcy that she's a good student, give Alec a great show, and experience this orgasm Darcy has been building me towards for what feels like hours.

"You going to do it for me?" Darcy asks. Her focus returns to my face, eyes dark with lust. "You going to show me what Rafael is talking about, soak my fingers then squeeze them, writhe underneath me, make more of those sexy sounds?"

I nod, unable to talk at this point, and Darcy keeps going, now past the moment where she'd previously left me hanging on the edge, approaching a sign saying: NO TURNING BACK. But we blew past that sign a while ago, probably when we kissed on the floor after Twister.

"I'm gonna," I warn, and her face breaks into this big grin, her head lowering by my ear.

She lowers her head near my ear and says, "Do it, Bex." Her voice urges me along with her fingers. "Come for me. Show me how gorgeous you are when you come apart."

Then, suddenly, her mouth is on my breast. My nipple between her teeth through the thin fabric of my swimsuit throws me over the edge.

I arch against the bed, groaning, and that's when I feel Darcy's fingers on my G-spot and *fuck*. This is level-ten stuff but Darcy does it like she's been doing it her whole life. A clitoral orgasm and a G-spot orgasm at the same time like it's no big deal. My fucking husband talked her through this, and I've never been more grateful for anything in my life, ever.

The orgasm lasts and lasts and lasts, and my body is pulsing and I'm flying and Darcy is saying things but I don't know exactly what, because her voice sounds like it's coming through a tunnel, from the other side of a long chasm.

Eventually, I collapse back against the bed. My breath is coming out in small pants, and my whole body is tingling. I could probably fall asleep right now, I'm so spent. It's been a long time since I crashed after an orgasm, but this wasn't just an orgasm, it was adrenaline like I've never experienced before. It was who-the-fuck-knows-what-else coursing through my veins, and now it's gone and I'm exhausted, eyes dropping closed.

"That was," I say sleepily, opening my eyes and seeing Darcy licking her fingers.

She presses her mouth to mine and I can taste myself on her.

"Fuck, that's hot," I murmur, and she laughs as my eyes flutter shut again. The endorphins carry me away and the rest of the world disappears–it's just me and this bed and Darcy's hand stroking my hair softly.

Chapter Fifteen

THE NEXT THING I know I'm still on Darcy and Alec's bed with Darcy, though she's sitting up, still stroking my hair lightly, as they talk about basketball. As if she didn't give me one of the best orgasms of my life—in front of our husbands.

"No way Mavs beat the Spurs to the playoffs," I say and when Darcy glances down at me, her face breaks into a grin.

"Hey there sleeping beauty."

"How long was I out?" I ask, pushing myself up to sitting.

"Not long, maybe half an hour?" Rafe answers.

I glance over at him, and his dick is back in his pants, though the bulge there suggests he didn't get the kind of relief I did.

"Sorry."

"Don't be sorry, you earned it," Alec pipes up from the other end of the room, and I feel my face flush warm.

"If anyone earned it, it was your wife," I say, glancing at Darcy, who laughs.

"I'll take the kudos," she says with a grin, and then before I can overthink it, I shift, moving over her and straddling her lap.

Looking down at her, I run my hands across her scalp, then sweep her hair behind her shoulders. "How about instead of kudos, I pay you back?"

She glances up at me and nods, then lifts her whole face in my direction.

"I'd like that."

Instead of replying with words, I kiss her, cupping her jaw with my hands and tilting her face in the direction I want.

She sighs against my mouth and any nerves that were building fade away. I've never done this before, but I'm among friends, and we've come this far. I might as well give it a shot.

I kiss my way down her body, stopping off at her tits like I wanted to earlier, scraping my teeth over the fabric of her suit, suckling though the fabric when her nipple makes itself known. Honestly, I want to peel her suit off and go after her, skin on skin, but there's something I want even more, so I keep moving lower.

The one-piece she's wearing tonight has a deep 'V' that goes almost to her bellybutton, so I kiss along that expanse of skin, making sure every exposed inch is attended to by my lips and teeth and tongue. She tastes salty, a reminder of how hard she worked to get me off, how many times she brought me to the edge and then back, how I can't fucking wait to do the same for her.

I peek up at her and she's laying there, gorgeous, eyes shut and hair fanned out on the pillow. I nip at the underside of her breast and her eyes open and she looks down at me. The smile she gives me warms my insides, reminds me that she brought us into this room, that she admitted to fantasizing about me. Maybe me asking what I want to ask isn't an unrealistic desire, maybe she'll be into it, maybe she'll say yes.

I kiss the top of her thigh. "I really want to know what you taste like."

The sharp intake of breath lets me know she's heard me, but the long pause after I ask makes me think she's not ready. Which is completely fair, and I refuse to take it personally.

I shift my approach. "Tell me, how do you want to get off? I want to make you feel as good as you made me."

"God, I want your mouth on me so fucking bad."

She looks shy, vulnerable, and when our eyes meet, she gets flustered. "I mean...is that not what you meant? Fuck, I've gone and made it awkward and..."

My laughter cuts her off and I just shake my head. "Darcy, I came all over your hand while our husbands watched. If that didn't make it awkward then I think we're good."

In the back of my head, though, there's a little voice telling me that we're fucked, and not in the good way. That our friendship has been torpedoed and there's no coming back from this. That in the morning we'll have tons of regret and won't be able to look each other in the eye.

But then the devil on my shoulder says that if all that's true, at the very least, I should make her come on my tongue before sunrise.

"That's exactly what I meant," I say, "Can I take your suit off, or do you want me to pull the crotch aside?" I ask, pressing my knee against said crotch and feeling her shift. She's damp and I just know that when I get to touch her, she'll be slick for me. When I peel her open and examine every crease and fold, she'll be glistening with her own juices. When I'm done using my mouth to make her squirm and whimper and—hopefully, if all goes to plan—come, my lips will be wet and taste like her pussy.

She glances over my shoulder to the corner where I know Alec is sitting, and I focus my attention on her breasts, so they can have whatever silent conversation they need in order to make sure everyone's onboard. I give Rafe a quick glance as well, and he wiggles his eyebrows in my direction.

I don't think I've ever loved this man more than I do at this very moment.

Darcy's voice cuts through my thoughts. "Guess I'm going to be the first of us to get naked."

My pussy clenches and there are so many possible reasons why. Maybe it's the fact that Darcy's about to get naked. Maybe it's the fact that I'm about to go down on her. Maybe it's the fact that she said *first*, implying that more of us will, if not tonight then before we go home, get naked. I suddenly want Darcy and Alec to watch Rafe and I fuck, I want to watch them fuck, I want to go down on Rafe while Darcy goes down on me and Alec goes down on her, I want to know if Rafe is a bottom or a top or a switch and I want to know the same for Alec. Even keeping to the limits we set earlier in this trip—before any of this seemed at all possible and it was just a hypothetical—even if Alec and I don't touch, and Rafe and Darcy don't touch, there are so many possible combinations that it makes my head spin. I want to experience them all and watch the ones I can't take part in.

But first I get to strip Darcy naked and eat her out.

She's already started pulling her straps down, and I love how eager she is for me, but I want to take my time, so I catch her hands, pinning them above her head, and slip my other hand between her legs. Even over the fabric I can tell how wet she is, but when I slide the crotch aside and run my thumb over the seam of her, I can tell she's so fucking ready.

"Bex," she says, and her voice is breathy, pleading. And honestly, if she hadn't teased me for what felt like forever I might have just dived right in and tried to break her all-time fastest orgasm record.

But she did, so I won't. Sorry not sorry, bestie.

"I'm going to let your hands go," I say, stroking her crease with lazy strokes, careful not to dip past the outer folds, get anywhere near her clit. "But I'm the one who gets to undress you, okay? You've tortured me so much this trip, the least you can do is let me have this."

She nods and when I let her go her body relaxes against the bed. I slide my fingers under the strap of her swimsuit and pull it down slowly, following afterwards with kisses that are sloppy on purpose, leaving a damp trail behind it. And I'm halfway down the second arm when the air conditioning kicks on and the trail breaks out in goosebumps at the temperature change.

Her nipples get hard too, and quick as I can I tug her suit far enough down to expose her tits because I want to taste those gorgeous peaks.

They're dusky pink and incredibly responsive to my mouth. Once I've had my fill of them, I continue the journey south. Kissing my way down to her navel, and then nibbling my way to her hips. I slide off the bed, kneeling at the end of it, and tug her closer to me.

I'm about to pull her swimsuit off entirely when I realize her breathing is a little faster, I see the thumb of her right hand cracking that hand's knuckles.

"Darcy?" I ask.

"I'm fine. Just nervous."

"Darcy," I say again, less of a question this time.

"I'm fine!" she insists.

But I don't believe her, so crawl back on the bed next to her and her breathing calms.

"What?"

"I couldn't see you," she admits. "You disappeared down there and suddenly it was like, what am I doing letting this non-Alec person go down on me?"

Hearing that hurts, but I focus on Darcy, not my feelings. So I swallow and nod, stroking her hair.

"Then we stop. Or we can do other things, non-oral things if you want. I'll do whatever things you want me to, Darcy, or nothing, if you need to call a time-out."

She shakes her head, then closes her eyes and takes a deep breath. "No time-out."

"But you just—" I start, but she cuts me off.

"You're not some random non-Alec person. You're Bex and as soon as you came back up here, I remembered that. I couldn't do it with a random, but you're anything but."

For the second time in as many hours, Darcy's confession leaves me feeling warm and soft. "Yeah?"

She nods, then leans up, and when I press my mouth against hers, she kisses me like she means it. Like she's dying of thirst and I'm a glass of water, like she's never going to get another chance. We break apart for air but after a gasp dive in again. She rolls to her side and slips a knee between my legs and soon we're both humping each other, seeking to release some of the aching need that's building.

Except I've already had a release tonight and she hasn't, so with effort I pull away. I slide to the foot of the bed again, kneel between her thighs, and plant a kiss where her suit meets her skin.

"What color is the sun, Darcy?"

I hear the smile in her voice when she answers. "Purple."

The color furthest from yellow on the color wheel. She's sure this time.

I give one last tug to her suit, and she's naked.

The room smells like Darcy, like sex, and as I kneel, eye-level with her, the musky smell of her is stronger.

I've never been this up close and personal with a pussy that isn't mine before, never been so exposed to a smell that isn't me. I'm not sure if it's a pheromone thing or the fact that I'm so fucking turned on right now. Maybe it's just the fact that it's Darcy and I've known her for years, lived with her for years, so everything about her already feels so familiar. Whatever it is, I fucking love it. It's so her, the smell, the musk, the everything permeating the air, so I nudge her legs a little further apart, spread her open so I can see her better, and drink it all in.

She's so pretty, a slightly darker shade of pink than I am, and fully bare, so fucking soft and smooth.

And wet. When I rub my thumb down the seam of her it's slick, It's not hard to find her clit, this solid little nub above her opening, and when I brush against it gently her whole body jolts.

I want to do it again and again and again, I want to make her writhe and gasp and moan, I want to fuck her with my fingers relentlessly. But I also want to take my time and draw it out for forever. Torture her a bit.

The latter wins, knowing that I'll get to do the former eventually, but that starting slow will probably be better for both of us. I pull her another couple of inches closer to me, so that the edge of her ass is just barely on the bed, and hook one of her legs over my shoulder, holding the other one open. She's propped herself up on her elbows, watching me, so I lock eyes with her and lean in to give her a slow, soft, lick.

She tastes the way she smells: musky, earthy. With my free hand I spread her open wider, trace my tongue along her folds, and her eyes widen a bit, face softening. My tongue traces the same path and she groans, flattening against the bed, and the eye contact breaks.

"Hey Alec," I say looking over my shoulder, and for the first time see his cock. He's got it in hand, stroking up and down. Our eyes meet and he doesn't look embarrassed or ashamed, just aroused, and really, isn't that basically the theme of the night?

"Up and down or side to side?" I ask, because Rafe and Darcy talking about how to get me off was one of the hottest things I've ever experienced, second only to this moment right here. Two people that love me—in different ways, yes, but love me nonetheless—crowdsourcing how to give me a mind-blowing orgasm? What kind of best friend would I be if I didn't do the same for her?

"Back and forth," he offers, licking his lips. "With the flat of your tongue against her clit. If you want to tease her—"

"If?" I interrupt, laughing. "Rafe, do you think I want to tease her?"

Rafe grins at Darcy.

"I don't think she'll have the patience tonight, but next time she'll tease you within an inch of your life," says my husband—who's rubbing himself through his pants again—to my best friend who's spread-out naked in front of me, her pussy juices all over my mouth.

"He's right," I admit. Teasing each other is what Rafe and I do, and if we're bringing Darcy and Alec into this relationship they should probably know that sooner rather than later.

Wait, are we bringing Darcy and Alec into this relationship?

I shake the question off, because it's an issue for future-Bex to worry about. Right-now-Bex is going to focus on Darcy instead.

"How do I tease her then?"

"Fuck her with your tongue."

The room is filled with a groan, but it's not the one I was expecting. It's one I know much more intimately. I glance over at Rafe again and his head is back against the wall, eyes closed, and he's reaching into his pants. Seeing me kneeling in front of Darcy's pussy didn't get him masturbating, but Alec's dirty talk does?

His thumb rubs over the head of his cock and then his hand slides along the shaft. He closes his eyes and I wonder if he's thinking about me or Alec or maybe both of us. Maybe I'm sucking him off while Alec fucks his ass, or maybe I sit on his face while Alec sucks him off. Any combinations of positions would be fantastic.

I squeeze my legs together and give Darcy another lick because she's where my focus is supposed to be.

Following Alec's suggestions, I flatten my tongue against her clit and move it back and forth. When she seems to be getting into it, when her lower half starts rocking against me, I switch to fucking her with my tongue. A minute or so of that and then I give her clit a few hard sucks, before starting over again from the beginning.

Soon it's taking less and less time for her to start squirming at each stage so I decide to mix it up and ease in a finger and she gasps.

"Fuck, Bex." I grin against her pussy, then turn my head and give her inner thigh a little nip with my teeth.

"Haven't even found your G-spot yet, save something for that."

A second finger joins the first, and after a minute or so of exploring I find a soft ridge. When I stroke that Darcy gasps. I stroke it again and Darcy almost arches off the bed, and I hear Alec from his corner.

"You found it?"

I glance over at him and he looks a little excited, hopeful.

"Yeah, you wanna try?"

In a flash he's tucked himself back into his pants and is kneeling next to me.

I'm slowly running my finger back and forth across it, and Darcy's squirming on the bed. "What the *fuck*," she gasps. "Seriously *what the fuck*?"

She seems to be enjoying it, but I'm not entirely sure, so I check in.

"Color?" I ask, and she just shakes her head rapidly.

"Literally any color on the spectrum except that one!"

With a laugh I kiss her inner thigh again, then switch from three fingers back down to one. A glance at Rafe to make sure this is okay and Rafe just nods, eyes darting back and forth between the two of us.

Darcy's squirming means that the leg that's slung over my shoulder keeps moving and I pin it against me as I nod towards her.

"Slip your finger in next to mine," I tell Alec. He does, tracing along the length until he finds the spot inside his wife that I'm stroking.

"There you go," I tell him. I slowly ease my finger out while he experiments, moving his finger up and down, back and forth, slipping in a second.

"Oh my God it's so much," Darcy whimpers, covering her face with her hands. "Fuck it's like an orgasm but it's not, it's different but, God, I could let you do this forever, fuck."

She whimpers our names, both of them—Alec and Bex, Bex and Alec—and I spread her top folds apart again and put my mouth to her, sucking her clit.

"Fuck!" she yells, actually *yells* and I just keep sucking as Alec keeps stroking and Darcy keeps writhing and swearing and yelling our names.

And then she's arched and still, letting out a string of swears.

A moment later she's limp against the bed.

I ease off the suction, placing a hand on Alec's wrist to ease off the stroking. Darcy's only sounds now are whimpers, her only movement is when she takes a breath.

Alec pulls back completely, crawling next to her on the bed, and I sit back on my heels, watching them as he strokes her face softly.

I guess it takes a few minutes for Darcy to find her voice, and when she does, she asks weakly, "What the fuck *was* that?"

I laugh, pressing a kiss to that gorgeous pussy of hers, and laugh again when she jolts at the contact. "G-spot orgasm. Your first?"

She nods and when I watch Alec there's no doubt in my mind that they're totally and completely besotted with each other. He's whispering something in her ear and she's laughing quietly and they're in their own little world, and maybe it would be normal to feel jealous or something, but I don't. If anything I feel proud, because I helped that moment of connection happen, because I showed him how to make her do that.

Besides, there's someone in this room that *I'm* completely besotted with, and I crawl across the floor of the room and settle between his feet, leaning my head against his knee.

"You were so fucking hot, B," Rafe says in my ear, and even though there's a gorgeous naked woman in the room, and even though I'm sure about the hunger I saw him direct toward Alec earlier, I believe him. Because what I did with Darcy didn't change how I feel about him, even an iota.

He runs his hand through my hair as I snuggle against him and I sigh, content. Because this evening has been weird as fuck—probably the weirdest I'll ever have in my life—but it's also been pretty fucking awesome.

"Love you," I say quietly, and when he looks at me there's adoration in his eyes.

"Love you too," he replies. "More than ever."

Chapter Sixteen

I WAKE UP AT five in the morning needing to pee, and can't get back to sleep.

"You okay, mi vida?" Rafe asks drowsily when he wakes up an hour later and catches me scrolling through my phone.

"Can't sleep," I say, eyes glued to the screen until I feel his hand on my hip, pulling me closer.

"You okay, though?" he repeats, and I tear my eyes away from my phone and look at him.

"I don't know. A little freaked out."

"Why?"

What a ridiculous question. "Why? Maybe because someone other than you made me come last night. Maybe because I made out with my best friend. Maybe because her fingers were in my pussy and my tongue was on her clit. How are you not freaking out right now too? Just a few hours ago your wife made out with someone other than you!"

"Because we talked about it before," he says, shrugging. "Because she checked with me every step of the way. Because she gave me no reason to question anything as far as our relationship goes. I got to watch her live out a fantasy, and two new people saw my wife for the gorgeous, sensual, sexy as fuck woman she is. Also, honestly, it's nice to know that they'll be forever jealous of me because I get her every night forever and ever, amen."

I just watch him for a moment, speechless, because what could I possibly say in response to that? But it helps me relax a tiny bit even though I don't know what this all means. To distract myself I shift right up against him, and give him a kiss.

"I love you," I say, and he looks down at me and gives me a kiss as well.

"I love you too."

Then we're kissing and I'm sliding on top of him and his hands are cupping my ass and my knees adjust so that I'm straddling him. I kiss the corner of his mouth, his jawline, his Adam's apple, his collarbone, and further and further down until I've trapped the waistband of his boxer briefs between my teeth and I'm tugging them down.

His cock jumps to life like it'd been lying in wait. I rush to tug his underwear all the way off then reach for him, wrapping my fingers around the base.

He groans.

"You," I say, licking him from root to tip. "Didn't get"—another lick—"to come"—lick—"last night, did you?"

By now he's fisting the sheets trying to restrain himself. He shakes his head as I capture one of his balls in my mouth, and he lets out a shaky breath.

"Do you want to?" I ask, and he laughs, thrusting lightly against my hand in response, because the answer is so obvious.

"Fine," I say, with a playful exasperation, and wrap my lips around his cock, swirling my tongue around the head before going lower.

Starting off slow, I lock eyes with him and he looks so intense and it's so fucking hot. I use my hands as an extension of what I can't reach with my mouth and his thrusts become faster, less controlled. My free hand cups his balls, plays with them, and then when I stroke the soft spot a few inches behind them, he groans.

"Rebecca," he says in that hoarse tone of voice that I love so much. "Fuck, you're so fucking good and your mouth is so wet and your hands are so good and I don't want to stop."

Then don't, I think, speeding up my pace. I love going down on him because I love the way he reacts to me. One of his hands moves from the sheets to my head, fisting my hair, and the other moves to the headboard, because his thrusts are making it lightly bang against the wall and he tries to push it quiet. Though I'm not sure the headboard is our biggest problem, because occasionally he lets out these guttural groans that shoot straight to my pussy.

He's speaking rapidly now, a mix of English and Spanish, and he's the sexiest guy on the planet when he's about to come, when he tugs my hair with every thrust, when his cock approaches the back of my tongue, when he's about to lose control and it's because of me.

Then one more jerk and he freezes, cum hitting the back of my mouth in hot splurts. The hand in my hair pulls me down so that his cock rests against my tongue, not quite hitting my gag reflex, and holds me there as his body stays tense, riding out his orgasm.

Then he sags against the bed, relaxed.

"Fuck," he says quietly and I laugh, crawling up the bed. The kiss he gives me is brief but his arms wrap around me, warm and secure.

"Good?" I ask, even though I know the answer, because who doesn't like hearing it?

"The best."

Then we hear a voice.

"Bex go down on you, or was that sex?" Alec calls through the wall, and I flush red even though I should be past that, and bury my face in Rafe's chest.

"Bex," Rafe calls, and I can hear the grin in his voice.

"Jealous," is Alec's response.

I pull away to glance at Rafe, and the look he's giving me is hungry. Possessive.

"Your dick isn't getting anywhere near my wife."

"That's not what I'm jealous of," is the reply.

Rafe blanches, slightly panicked, but I also feel his cock coming back to life. I raise my eyebrows at him silently and he just looks away.

"Might be able to negotiate something," I call, and Rafe lets out a breath I didn't realize he'd been holding. "Let's discuss terms later."

"Sounds like a deal."

Rafe glances at me, forehead knotted, and I stand up and reach my hand out for him. Tugging him into the bathroom, I start the shower.

"You don't have to do anything you don't want to. You know that, right?"

He nods.

"Is the problem that you want to?"

I see his Adam's apple bob in a swallow, and he gives the tiniest nod.

"So I guess the question is..."

He groans, resting his forehead against mine.

"I'm about to get my comeuppance, aren't I? For asking you a dozen times yesterday."

I grin. "My non-answer was an answer in and of itself, though. So, do you want me to talk you into it, or out of it?"

He doesn't answer, instead hoists me on the counter, nudges my legs apart, and drops to his knees in front of me.

A non-answer.

"I'll accept this response," I say, looking down at him, and he looks back with obvious thanks as he pulls me right to the edge of the counter then covers me with his mouth. We can wait until later to discuss whether or not he wants his best friend to blow him.

Chapter Seventeen

WE'RE THE FIRST ONES in the kitchen this morning, and I'm halfway through my cereal when Darcy and Alec come out of their room.

"I've decided we're not going to be awkward about this," Darcy declares. "Putting it out there, last night was really fun, and I'd like to do it again, but if you don't, just say the word. We can pretend it never happened. I just want to make sure all four of us are on the same page."

I glance at Rafe, who shrugs to indicate it's up to me, so I look back at Darcy.

"I don't think we have to pretend like it didn't happen."

"Which means?" she prods, and this time it's my turn to shrug.

"Bex!" she exclaims. "Please don't make me do this all on my own here."

"I don't know how to do this!"

"I don't either!"

"You're just the one who usually takes charge," I point out. Darcy chews her lip and I realize the bravado from a moment ago was false, was 'fake it till you make it.'

"Please," she says quietly, though loud enough that all of us can hear her. "I just... if it's just me that's into it that's fine, but if it's not then I need to hear you say it."

I swallow, and under the table Rafe's hand covers my knee, thumb stroking my skin soothingly.

"It isn't," I finally say. "This is all so weird but..." I swallow again. "A vacation fling would be fun."

Darcy breaks into a grin. "It's because I'm so good at getting you off, isn't it," she says, reaching out and dragging her finger down my arm, and I roll my eyes, cheeks heating, and bury my face in my hands. The other three laugh, but it's a laughter of comradery.

I peek at them through my fingers. "I mean it's not *not* because of that," I say, and Rafe wiggles his eyebrows at me and Darcy looks incredibly pleased with herself and Alec whistles. "But first," I say over the laughter, "the beach. I need to recover from this morning."

"After the blowjob? Shower?" Darcy asks, glancing at our bedroom door, and I nod. She crosses her arms and gives an exaggerated pout, and I just give her a coy look.

"Maybe if you're lucky, later..."

Then I stop and glance at Alec. "Sorry, this is weird! You're her husband!"

But Darcy ignores the distraction, focusing on her shot at the shower. "If I'm lucky later?"

I stand up and walk around the table to her, cup my hand around her ear and whisper quietly enough that only she can hear, "Maybe if you're lucky later I'll fuck you with my fingers while I point the handheld at your clit."

When I pull away, she's looking at me, slightly stunned, but in a very flattering way. "Bex, fuck," she says.

But I refuse to let myself feel self-conscious about it, and instead brush my lips against hers lightly. I'm pulling away when her hand wraps around my neck and pulls me to her, parting my mouth with her tongue. I push her two steps backwards and her back hits the door frame. She wraps an arm around my waist and pulls my hips against hers. And then we're full-on making out, tongues warring, hands wandering, thighs rubbing up against crotches. It isn't until we're short of breath that we pull away, glance at each other, and then burst out laughing.

"I've got to go before I take her right here on the kitchen floor," I say, grabbing Rafe's hand.

"I'm actually okay if you—" he starts, and I wag my finger at him tugging him to the bedroom to change.

"Hush," I laugh. "Or you won't get to watch tonight."

He hushes.

***

For obvious reasons, the beach feels different today. When we lay our things out and I pull off my cover-up I catch Darcy watching me with open admiration. Grinning, I gesture to her. She tosses her hair back and pulls her kaftan over her head, slowly revealing swaths of skin. Some of it's covered by her suit, but I've seen her naked, know what's there, have kissed what's there.

"Like what you see?" She asks like she's teasing, but I see the hint of insecurity under the airs.

So I lean forward and give her a quick kiss, something chaste and public-appropriate, and squeeze her thigh briefly. "I really do."

And the way she brightens up is proof that I read her right, that she needed a little bit of a confidence boost.

Which, frankly, blows my mind.

"Do you really not know you're gorgeous?" I ask, and she shrugs. "Does Alec not tell you, like, all the time?"

"Alec's different," she says. "He's legally obligated to think I'm hot."

"He's actually not," I point out. "I was there, none of your vows said anything about 'and you must always think each other hot.'"

"You know what I mean though, right? Like a hot guy at the grocery store checking you out is more exciting than Rafael doing it, right? Or a different kind of exciting?"

"Yeah, I guess. I mean—" I start, and then realize what she said and glance over at her, surprised. "Wait, am I the hot guy at the supermarket?"

She laughs and nods and hands me the sunscreen, turning her back to me.

"You know, you're supposed to put this on before you leave the house," I say, slathering it on her. "It's more effective if you give it time to work."

"Yeah, but if I ask you to do it then I have an excuse to get your hands all over me."

I laugh but slow down, slipping my hands under her straps, making sure the lotion is fully rubbed in with no white streaks. Then I slide my hands over her shoulders, down her front, stopping right above her breasts and then changing my focus to her arms.

"Bex," she says quietly, and I don't know what the look on her face is because I'm behind her, but her voice is nothing but heat.

I bet her eyes are, too.

"Hmmm?" I ask, feigning innocence and she shakes her head.

"Asshole."

"Don't think we're there yet."

She pulls away and lays down, glancing up at me. "Speaking of which. What's going on with the guys?"

An image flashes in my mind of Alec naked, bent over the bed, jerking himself off as Rafe slides in slowly from behind.

Darcy's voice cuts into my thoughts. "You're thinking about them."

I roll my eyes, but nod.

"Your tits are a dead giveaway, every time."

I glance down and see that, as noted, my nipples are hard, poking through my swimsuit.

"Exactly how long have you been checking out my boobs to figure out my horniness?"

"Longer than I should admit," she says, and her face pinks up.

I laugh, and then without thinking, I lean over to kiss her.

It's just a quick kiss, the kind of peck I give Rafe when we're laughing over a shared joke, and it feels so easy, so natural. But when I pull away, I see the surprise on her face, and mine heats.

"Sorry," I mumble, looking away as I pull my hair into a ponytail.

"Don't be," she says, and her shoulder bumps against mine. When I chance a glance at her, she's smiling, though it's a shy one. It's weird, because Darcy is never shy, especially not around me.

But I also like it.

"I was just surprised," she continues. "I'm not used to casual kisses with anyone but Alec. I'm not used to any kind of kisses with anyone but Alec. But I... I like it," she shrugs, "with you."

"Same," I say. "Both the 'not used to kissing anyone but Rafe' and the liking it. With you."

She grabs my hand and lays down, tugging me down next to her, and we watch the clouds, lying next to each other with our fingers entwined.

"Have you and Alec talked about it? Him and Rafe, I mean."

She nods. "Your husband is hot, you know."

"He is," I agree with a laugh.

"You two?"

I hesitate a moment, wondering if I shouldn't answer, if I should let Rafe decide for himself whether or not to tell them. But I feel like he wouldn't mind. Not after how weird this week has gotten anyway. "Yeah. There's definitely an interest, but..."

"He just came out," Darcy supplies, and I nod.

"Did you know? Or suspect?"

I shake my head. "I mean, I'm fine with it, obviously. But I was surprised. I think it was more about him not admitting it to himself. If he's not ready to say it to himself, of course he's not going to say it to me."

"What do you think made him change his mind?"

"I'm not sure," I admit. "Maybe it's because we were just talking about it so openly. Maybe it's because he was just ready. Maybe because..."

I stop suddenly, flushing, and Darcy raises her eyebrows with curiosity.

"Maybe because...?" she prompts, and I shrug, pretending like it's not a big deal.

"Maybe because my crush on you had come up and it made him willing to acknowledge his crush on Alec."

"Your crush on me!" she says, looking very pleased with herself.

I laugh, elbowing her gently but giving her hand a squeeze. "Shut up," I say but she keeps preening.

Then she props herself up on her elbow, leans over, and gives me a kiss. This one lingers a moment longer than my earlier one, but it's still chaste.

My nipples disagree, though.

Darcy sees them and laughs.

"Shut up," I say again, covering myself with my arm and laughing. Our laughs mingle as she shakes her head, doing a little shimmy of her shoulders, obviously pleased that my nipples are so fond of her.

I roll my eyes, but it's all in good fun, and I love how natural and easy and familiar this all feels. As if we've been doing this forever. How in the world is it supposed to end at the end of the vacation? We're really meant to just go back to how things were? It feels impossible.

I push the thought away, focusing on right now. On how good right now feels.

Chapter Eighteen

Later that afternoon Rafe pulls me into the water, letting me know it's my turn to get off in the ocean, and when his fingers slip into my suit and then my pussy, I wrap my arms around his shoulders, burying my face into the crook of his neck. Then he massages my G-spot, and I need to keep my mouth occupied to keep from groaning, moaning, gasping, and by the time I've come there's another hickey where his neck meets his shoulder, a bruise—red turning purple, faint teeth marks around it.

"Sorry I'm not sorry," I say.

He grins, rubbing the spot absently. "How bad is it?"

I shrug. "Hardly noticeable."

"Holy shit, how do I get one of those?" Darcy asks when we return to the towels.

Rafe looks over at me. "Hardly noticeable?"

"From a spaceship, maybe," Alec says.

Darcy considers that. "Pretty sure the ISS can, actually, see it."

"Shut up," I say, leaning over to shove her, but she grabs my hand before I do, weaving our fingers together.

"Nah."

When we get back to the Airbnb we rinse off in the shower, and for once Rafe and I don't get it on, instead just have a few quick kisses before pulling on clothes and heading back out into the living room.

Darcy and Alec have beaten us to it, and now they're putting on a show. Alec sits in one of the armchairs, legs spread, one arm resting along the armrest, while the other is tangled in Darcy's hair as she kneels between his legs. He guides her head up and down, up and down, and even though I can't see her mouth or his cock it might be the hottest thing I've ever seen. His eyes are closed, but Rafe makes a quiet noise and Alec opens them, and when he sees us, he smirks.

God, he's hot. No wonder Rafe wants him.

Taking my hand, Rafe moves us slightly. We're at an angle now where we can see the action, Alec's cock disappearing into Darcy's mouth, and then reappearing, glistening. He pulls her hair back so that none of it is in the way, and when his fist tightens again, she whimpers and I feel my pussy clench. It's the same sound she made last night when my teeth closed around her nipple, the mix of pleasure and pain.

She doesn't stop though, head bobbing up and down his cock, one hand cupping his balls, massaging. I'm not even sure if she knows we're there, though, not until I can hear Alec's voice in a tone quiet enough that it's obviously meant for her, but still loud enough for us to be able to make out.

"Sweetheart, we have company," he says. "And Bex is looking at you so hungrily I wouldn't be surprised if you told me you can feel her eyes on you. You were right, her nipples did poke out."

I laugh and cover my face, because how did this become a Thing, while Rafe wraps an arm around my tits, shielding them from view. He pulls my back against his front and I can feel the hint of an erection starting as I nestle against his chest.

"Stop looking at my wife's tits," he says good-naturedly.

When Alec replies, however, it's all heat. "Any place else I should look instead?"

Rafe's breath goes ragged, his heart pounding against my back, and his arm stiffens against me. Alec's looking right at him, and when I glance up at my husband his eyes are locked on Alec's.

Then he breaks eye contact, looking down at me. I see guilt in his eyes." Sorry," he says.

I shake my head, turning towards him and pulling his mouth down to mine. "Don't be," I say before kissing him. "Look wherever you want."

Then I wrap my arms around his midsection, resting my forehead on his shoulder and closing my eyes. Giving him permission, and hoping it helps him be less self-conscious about whatever he chooses.

Rafe's arm winds around my back, and slowly his heart becomes less frantic.

Then it speeds up, his breath going ragged, and the hand at my back fists my shirt. The noises behind me are becoming sloppier, and I hear Alec breathe faster, slurping sounds from Darcy.

"Do you want to watch him come?" Rafe whispers, and I nod, so he turns me around, pulling him against him. That's when I realize he's gone rock hard, tenting his gray sweatpants. Darcy's moving quickly now, Alec thrusting into her mouth as his hand pulls her down on him.

And he's still staring at my husband. I don't dare look at Rafe, so instead I just hope he's too turned on to be self-conscious, instead just taking in the incredibly hot picture of Alec fucking Darcy's mouth as Darcy's hand is down her...

Holy shit, how did I miss that? Because her free hand is down her pants and I can't see much but I can see enough to tell that it's rubbing, that she's getting herself off as she gets Alec off and I don't think this scene could be any hotter.

Then she groans around his dick, the sound muffled but still clear, it's a variation of what we've heard throughout the weekend, of her orgasm. There's a whimper and her mouth stops moving but her hand moves a little more furiously before a loud moan, and Alec reaches down, grabbing another fistful of her hair, and thrusting upwards, once, twice, three times, before freezing with a groan of his own.

His eyes are still trained on Rafe, and Rafe's whole body is moving with his breaths, moving mine as well.

Then Rafe speaks quietly in my ear. "I need a minute, mi vida. Going to disappear into our room, don't come after me, okay?"

I nod and he lets go of me, pressing a kiss to my temple, and slipping into our bedroom, closing the door behind him.

"Everything okay?" Darcy asks. She's collapsed on the floor, stretched out with her arms above her head, in a way that makes her tits look mouthwatering. But I try not to stare—she deserves some time to recuperate. So instead, I nod, moving to sit next to her.

"Think he just needs a minute."

I rub a strand of her hair between my fingers as she nods, glancing up at me with a smile.

When I lean over to kiss her, I taste Alec on her. It's the first time I've tasted a guy other than Rafe in so long, and it brings back the weirdness of what we're doing. The surrealness of the fact that Darcy and I are spending the week hooking up, that our husbands might too.

If Rafe gets comfortable with the idea. If he decides it's worth the risk.

"Too much?" Alec asks.

I glance over at him, then shake my head. "Super hot."

"I just don't want to freak out..." He juts his chin in the direction of our closed bedroom door.

I shake my head again. "I don't think you are. If he reaches a point where he's had enough, he'll make it known. Just now, if he wanted to watch Darcy, he'd have watched Darcy. If he wanted to turn it into a parallel play situation, he'd have asked. He knows I'd have dropped to my knees for him."

Darcy makes a needy noise at that and I give her hair a gentle tug. "Not the point, Darcy."

"But can it be?"

I chuckle, leaning over to give her another quick kiss. Alec leans over to pull her feet into his lap, rubbing the arch of her foot with his thumb.

She sighs, content. "Okay, this'll do for now."

"Are you going to check on him?" Alec asks and I shake my head, shifting so that I'm closer to Darcy's head, running my fingers through her hair and lightly scratching her scalp. Her eyes flutter shut and I can't help but grin at how at peace she looks. Relaxed enough that she might just melt into the floor. I love this, love how she looks. Love that I'm part of the reason.

"Nah, he asked me not to. If I had to guess, he's probably getting himself off and doesn't want me there because I'm not who he's thinking of."

I give Alec a meaningful look and the expression that crosses his face is unlike any I've seen from him before—a bashful sort of pride, with a glimmer of hope.

"I honestly don't know if it'll go anywhere," I add. I feel bad, because I don't want to crush his hopes, but I also don't quite have a read on where Rafe's head is at. "We've only got tonight and tomorrow night left. It may not be enough time for him to get comfortable with the idea."

I don't add that when the trip is over, whatever this is, is over too.

He nods. "You're right."

The tone of his voice makes it obvious, though, what he's hoping for. He wants this, wants Rafe. "Whatever happens, it's fine with me, I'm obviously only interested in moving forward if he's fully on board," he says.

Which is when the door to our bedroom opens. Rafe appears, takes a deep breath, and without saying anything crosses the room.

When he reaches us, he leans over, and grabs Alec's jaw. Then, silently, Rafe kisses him.

Chapter Nineteen

DARCY LOOKS AT ME and I look back, both our eyes wide because holy fuck, Rafe just kissed Alec. Alec grabs a fist full of Rafe's shirt, pulling him closer. Rafe turns his head sideways, opening his mouth, and I see a flash of tongue as Alec does as well. Alec stands and Rafe hauls him closer. And suddenly they're actively making out, grasping hair and limbs and clothes.

Rafe grabs at the hem of Alec's shirt, tugging upwards, and when they pull apart to remove it, Alec gasps, "Darcy's okay with whatever."

"Bex too," Rafe says, and suddenly there's an ugly feeling in the pit of my stomach because, am I? Am I really?

It's hypocritical, I know, but talking about them making out and actually watching your husband kiss someone else are two totally different things. I thought I was okay, but what if I'm not, what if I'm jealous, what if I'm not as good a person as Rafe is? Because if I asked him to stop, he would, there's no question in my mind about that, but can I ask? Is it okay to be unsure?

"Bedroom?" Rafe asks, and Alec nods, and I know we're supposed to follow them but I'm still sitting on the floor, frozen.

It's Darcy's voice that brings me back to earth. Her voice and her touch. A hand on my arm, another on my knee, a gentle squeeze.

"You okay?"

I nod, robotically, because I know that's what I'm supposed to answer, and then her hand strokes my cheek, turning me to look at her.

"Do you need to safe out?" she asks, and I shake my head because, again, that's what I'm supposed to answer.

"Do you want me to?" she presses, because she's my best friend and can read me like a book.

I hesitate, and she takes a deep breath as if to call out to the guys, but I shake my head, whispering, "No, don't."

"He'd want you to if you need to," she says simply, and I know it's true. They'd both want me to, neither would be okay with continuing if any of the four of us were uncomfortable.

"I know, I just... I don't know if I need to. I just need a second to process."

Darcy nods silently and waits, lacing our fingers together.

"It's weird," she says after a moment of silence.

"Yeah."

"It also feels hypocritical to say that," she adds, and I nod.

"Are you okay with it?" I ask after a beat. "Like really, truly, completely okay with it?"

She shrugs. "I don't know. Like, what does 'okay with it' mean, really? Do I love watching it? Part of me yes, part of me no. There's definitely a part of me that's jealous as fuck. But Alec was too, you know. Last night."

"Oh?"

She nods. "I think it's the fact that you found my G-spot. We've never spent a lot of time trying to find it, but still, you found it in, like, minutes."

I nod, and even with all these conflicting feelings swirling in me, there's a bit of pride.

"But I'm not going to leave him for you," she says with a grin, and I laugh.

"I don't expect you to."

"Exactly."

It takes a second for the meaning to sink in and then I roll my eyes. "Yeah, yeah."

"I'm serious though," she says, resting her hand on my thigh and her head on my shoulder. "Because isn't that what jealousy is partially about? That we're afraid they're going to like someone else better than us. That they're going to leave us for someone else. But I'm not. And you're not. And Alec isn't."

I nod, knowing she left the last person off intentionally. So that I'd say it. "And Rafe isn't."

"You're still allowed to safe out, though. It's why we set the word up, so that there's no guilt, no frustration, none of that."

"I want him to have this though," I say, and it's true, because I do.

"Would not watching help, then? We could just cuddle on the couch. Or more than cuddle on the couch," she adds, slowly dragging the hand that's on my thigh higher, and I laugh.

"I'd love to do that," I admit. "But I also think I want to watch? I'm just..."

"Weirded out," she says as she stands, and I nod, taking her hand and following her tug to standing. "Then we'll go watch, but if you want to tap out without safeing out... just let me know."

When we enter the bedroom Alec and Rafe are lying on the bed, still just kissing, but with far less clothing. Rafe's shirt is at the foot of the bed, and he's just wearing his sweatpants, while Alec is finishing pulling off his boxers, fully naked.

Rafe has Alec's cock in his hand, running a finger down the length of it, studying it carefully. I assume it's the closest he's come to one that isn't his, and he looks a little intimidated.

I understand why.

"Damn," I say to Darcy under my breath, and she wraps an arm around my waist, pulling me closer so her mouth is right up against my ear.

"Didn't call him coke-can Alec the first time we hooked up for nothing," she teases.

"Well, yes, but I thought you were exaggerating!"

"Me? Exaggerate? Never!"

I laugh, turning my head and giving her a quick peck before turning back to the guys. "Oh, there he goes."

And sure enough, Rafe has wrapped his hand around Alec's cock, first with a slow glide, and then speeding up just a tad. But then he stops and glances at me, and I can tell from the way he's looking at me, it's a practical question that he has.

"One sec," I say, standing up and digging through our bag, then tossing him a bottle of lube. He grins at me before he lubes Alec's cock up and then gives a quick pump of his hand.

"Fuck," Alec groans, and Rafe laughs and gives him another pump of his hand. Alec reaches up for him, pulls him down, and then they're kissing while Rafe jerks Alec off.

"God," Darcy says, resting her head against my shoulder, and I nod. My chest is flushed, my body tight, as the scene in front of me turns me on. My husband jerking off another guy turns me on. Maybe I'm not jealous at all, maybe I can be detached from it all, because who wouldn't want to watch two admittedly gorgeous men get it on right in front of them. Also, I'm proud of Rafe for taking a chance here.

And for the sounds he's bringing out of Alec.

Alec plants one foot flat on the bed, bending the other knee up, so that he can better thrust against Rafe's hand, and the kissing stops as he pants, needy noises escaping occasionally.

"I'm gonna," Alec gasps. "Is it okay if I... If you want to stop I can..."

"Nu-uh," Rafe says, in a demanding voice I know all too well. "You better not fucking stop. You better fucking come for me. You think I got you this close only to let you get the credit? I don't fucking think so."

"Holy shit," Darcy says under her breath, and I can't help but grin. "Rafe? Really?"

"Yep," I say, watching him and letting my head rest against hers, which is still nestled on my shoulder. "It's great."

"Yeah," she says, clearing her throat and shifting slightly from her spot on the floor. "Who knew that'd do it for me?"

"Yeah?" I ask, resting my hand on her knee, and she nods, clearing her throat again. Slowly I slide my hand up her leg, pulling her thighs apart, and she laughs.

"Stop distracting me, we're supposed to be watching your husband jerk mine off!"

"Fine," I whine quietly, "After, then."

"It's a deal," she says breathlessly. "But watch, he's about to come. I know that groan."

I keep my hand wrapped around her upper thigh, but redirect my focus back to the bed, where Rafe's giving Alec's cock a single pump of his hand, then waiting and saying something, then another pump. Alec's lips are moving too, and I don't know what he's saying, but the way that he's thrusting up against Rafe's hand gives us the gist of it.

"Rafe may not let him," I whisper to Darcy, but she shakes her head.

"Trust me, it's happening."

And she's right, because before I even realize what's happening Rafe is the one on his back, Alec's forearm against Rafe's chest and pinning him to the bed, and Alec is fucking his hand.

It's so fucking hot, and I can feel my nipples pebbling against my bra, my body full of the want that's been present this whole vacation. Alec is nodding, smirking, crushing his mouth against Rafe's and then he grunts and rests his forehead against Rafe's as he gives a few more thrusts, these shakier. Then a long exhale and he rolls off Rafe, flopping on his back on the bed next to him.

Rafe's body is shaking and I hear his unmistakable chuckle as he reaches for a discarded shirt and wipes his hand and the sheets off with it, before passing it on to Alec.

"Told you," Darcy says, and I can hear the grin in her voice. "Power games with Alec always end like that."

"I'd like to see a few more experiments around that 'always' theory," I say, "for science."

Darcy laughs, but nods. "For science."

Chapter Twenty

"YOUR HUSBAND'S REALLY ANNOYING," Alec says to me, once they've cleaned up, and I laugh and nod.

"I wasn't sure if he'd let you come," I reply.

"Sometimes you just have to take your orgasm, you know?"

"I'm pretty familiar with trying to eke an orgasm out of Rafe, yeah."

"I always make it worth the effort," Rafe argues, and I can't help but agree.

After he's recovered, I wonder if we're done, but Alec pulls Rafe so that he's sitting at the edge of the bed, then tugs off Rafe's sweatpants. Rafe laughs again, a joyful belly laugh, but the sound dies on his lips as Alec sinks to his knees and hooks his fingers over Rafe's boxers.

"You can always—" Darcy starts.

But I shake my head, cutting her off as Rafe nods at Alec, and Alec drags his boxers down. "I want this for him. For them. For all of us, really."

Because here's the thing—when Rafe okayed Darcy fingering me, okayed me going down on her, he gave me a gift. He let me explore this part of me that I'd never be able to explore with him, and everything he does with Alec is something he wouldn't be able to do with me. So I want this for him.

But I'm still glad I have Darcy to hold my hand.

Rafe looks down at Alec, who's planting open-mouthed kisses along Rafe's shaft, then switches to using his tongue, tracing the length of him. Alec looks up at Rafe, and I can tell that they're watching each other as Alec takes the head of Rafe's cock into his mouth.

Rafe's breath is getting choppy now, and I can hear it through the quiet of the room, how he holds it as Alec slides down his length and lets it out when he's back up at the tip. Rafe's hand reaches up to stroke Alec's hair as Alec slides up again, and then there's less breath holding as the pace quickens, though they're still staring at each other, clocking every movement.

But then, when I can tell by the tension in his body that he's close to coming, he looks at me, equal parts aroused and concerned.

"Kiss me?" he asks, and he really does say it like a question, like he's not sure if I want to. As if he's afraid that watching him, watching this, has changed how I feel about him.

It's all I can do to not run to him.

I kneel next to him on the bed, wrap my arms around his neck and kiss him deeply. I tell him I love him, tell him how fucking hot he is, this is.

"Yeah?" he asks, and I laugh and nod and kiss him again.

"So fucking hot."

His hand reaches up to graze my nipples, and they're hard against his fingers, confirming my words. I want to pull his mouth down to them, to have his tongue lavish me with attention as Alec sucks him off, but maybe there'll be an opportunity to do that another time. Right now, the focus should be on him and Alec.

So I look down at Alec who's working Rafe's cock like he was made for it.

"He's going to come soon," I tell Alec. "You ready for him?"

Alec nods, then goes down so deep on Rafe's cock that Rafe's eyes go wide. It's an expression I've never seen, not during oral, and then Alec does it again, and again, and Rafe is panting in a way that's new, a way I've never heard before, and the jealousy starts creeping in again. But I'm going to focus on my husband and his impending orgasm and not my own feelings.

"Are you going to come for Alec, babe? Are you going to let go so he can taste you, so he can suck you dry?" I move my mouth right by his ear, and then whisper, though it's loud enough that Alec can hear, so he gets the warning. "I want to see you fuck Alec's mouth. Do it for me, babe, fuck his mouth for me."

Rafe looks at me and nods, then grasps Alec's hair with both hands, fingers winding into the strands. Alec whimpers, and we both glance down at him, concerned, but he winks at Rafe to signal he's okay. And I swear, the hottest guy I know in real life winking at the man I love more than I've loved anyone, ever, is almost too much and I let out an involuntary groan. It might be the closest I've ever come to orgasming without being touched.

Then, as if I'm not hot and bothered enough, Rafe starts fucking Alec's mouth. I never thought he was holding back with me, but he must have been, because this is so much rougher. He shoves Alec down and holds him there, then lets him up for just a second before shoving him down again. My nipples get painfully tight, the skin of my breasts feeling stretched as far as they can go, and my panties are so damp they might have left a wet stain on my shorts because I'm so fucking turned on by this, by Alec going down on Rafe.

And I can tell that Alec is loving every second of it, that he loves nothing more than Rafe's cock sliding down his throat and then back out, than Rafe tugging on his hair, than Rafe's ass lifting up from the bed with every thrust.

Apparently, our love for Rafe's dick is something Alec and I have in common.

"I'm," Rafe says, and he's looking at me again, and I can tell that he's a little torn. I've been the only other person to make him come for over a decade and a half, and that's about to change. Knowing that is weird as fuck.

So I stroke his hair, kiss his forehead. Then whisper, "Will you look at him for me? I want to see you two looking at each other. I want your eyes on him when you come."

It was what he needed to hear, because he looks at Alec and Alec looks at Rafe. I see Rafe's knuckles go white because that's how hard he's gripping Alec's hair. He shoves his cock far into Alec's mouth, making a noise I'm incredibly familiar with. His body flexes in a way that I know intimately and he comes.

I have to admit, it's a little weird. Hot, yes. And I love how happy Rafe looks as he drops to his knees and kisses Alec. I slip off the bed to give them a moment, but I still read his lips as he tells Alec he can't believe he did that, and laughs when Alec asks him what he did exactly, since Alec is the one who did all the work.

I'm trying to figure out how I feel when Darcy's fingers wrap around mine, tugging me towards her. I follow the tug, settling next to her on the floor and she gives my thigh a squeeze then leaves it there, rubbing her thumb against my skin.

We don't say anything as the guys cuddle a bit and talk a bit. We just sit there in silence, and I rest my head against her shoulder until she turns her head to me, pressing a kiss against my forehead. "You know I love you, right?"

I nod, because I do know.

"Even so, even considering how much I love you, and even considering the amazing orgasm you gave me, and even considering the fact that you found my G-spot and then taught my husband how to find it. Even with all that..."

I pull my head off her shoulder and look at her, pulling the leg she isn't caressing up against my chest. She fixes me with a tender expression.

"Nothing we've done has changed how I feel about him."

I take a minute to let that sink in, and then lean forward to give her a quick kiss. "Same on all counts." I grin, then add, "Well, except the G-spot part."

She laughs. "Here's hoping I can pay it forward before the week's up."

Darcy just said the thing that all of us are thinking but none of us have been willing to say since it began. We're only two days—after today only one more night—away from the end of the week.

I don't want to think about how soon this will all be over, so instead I straddle Darcy's lap. Her hands cup my backside and mine cup the back of her neck, and I kiss her, tangling my fingers in her hair. She gasps against my mouth and I chuckle, then work my way down her neck, settling at her pulse point.

"Bex," she says, and I swear, even with a dozen weeks I don't think I'd get used to hearing her saying my name like that, in that tone of voice. It affects me so fucking much, and all I want is to hear it over and over again, as her hands grip my hair so hard it makes me wince or her nails claw at my back.

But right now, her hands just slide up and down my thighs slowly, almost lazily.

"You know you're the only one of us that hasn't gotten off."

"You going to fix that for me?" I ask, and my boldness surprises me because, even though I've known her forever, this thing that we're doing right now is new.

But also, it's Darcy, and even though this is new nothing else about our relationship is. So I know she's going to laugh and nod, going to slide her hands a little higher until they're cupping my ass, then further up until my shirt is coasting up my body, over my head, and gets tossed to the side. Her hands trace my bra and then her mouth follows, planting open-mouthed kisses on the curves of my breasts as her hands slide to my back and unhook my bra, and it joins my shirt on the floor.

"There they are," she murmurs, and I laugh, because she's right, my nipples are hard, eager for attention.

And she gives it to them, one getting her mouth while the other gets stroked and fondled and lightly pinched. Then she swaps and the cool air from the vents mix with her warm hand as her mouth moves to the other one.

"Mmmm," I sigh, hand stroking her hair as my body softens under her attention, easing its way into that wonderful combination of relaxation, of arousal, of comfort and desire.

Eventually her mouth makes its way back up to mine, and I kiss her back eagerly. The tension begins to build as her hands fumble with my shorts. I slide off her lap and she tugs them down, taking my underwear along with them.

I'm naked under Darcy's gaze. And Rafe and Alec's, if they're paying attention.

A quick glance at them confirms that they are. Rafe wiggles his eyebrows and I grin back, just as Darcy whispers, "Can I go down on you, Bex?"

My heart starts galloping as I look at her and nod, and she gives me a shy smile.

"I've never done this before," she admits, even though I know that.

"All of this is new territory for all of us but Alec," I remind her, reaching over and swiping all her hair over one shoulder, playing with the strands. "No pressure, no rush, and you can tap out whenever you want, even if I haven't come."

She nods. "Same to you. No pressure, no rush, and you can tap out if you get tired of me fumbling around down there."

I laugh and nod, leaning over to brush my lips against hers, and when I pull away, she wraps her hand around my neck and tugs me in for another kiss, deeper, more passionate.

"Deal," she says, then looks over at the guys, who are watching us eagerly. "Couple of pillows?"

They toss her three, and she motions for me to lie back, then slides them under my backside and nudges my legs open. A moment later I'm spread out, on display for everyone, pussy at a more comfortable level for her.

She takes a deep breath, and then her fingers spread my folds open. One of them brushes against my clit.

I jolt at the sensation and she laughs, but when she does it again, I'm ready and this time I sigh. Then I feel a kiss on my upper leg, followed by the warm wetness of her mouth on me.

I relax under her attention and her tongue starts mimicking the movement that her fingers have already learned. She's hesitant at first, but when I breathe her name I can tell her confidence builds, the pressure becomes a little firmer, the movements a little surer.

"Darcy," I gasp, reaching down for her hair, urging her against me. "More. Faster."

She listens, her movements increasing. When my fingers tighten against her scalp, she groans, the vibrations against my clit making me writhe.

Two decades of friendship means she's heard me talk about how sometimes I need a little roughness to push me over the edge, and she uses that knowledge. Her lips wrap around my clit and she sucks, pressure slowly increasing as one finger, then two, fuck me a little faster, and I start to come apart.

"I'm gonna," I say, but it's all I can manage because that's when my orgasm hits me—pleasure coursing through my veins as my thighs squeeze her head, my pussy clenching around her fingers.

I'm arched against the floor, heaving, when I come back to myself, and all the tension leaves my body as I slump against the plush area carpet.

"Damn."

"Good?" Darcy asks, crawling up my body, now that she's been freed from the viselike grip of my legs.

"Ehhh." I make a so-so motion with my hand and Darcy laughs, kissing me.

We join the guys on bed, and Rafe wraps his arms around me as Darcy and Alec snuggle.

"That was so fucking hot," I tell him, and his grin is equal parts self-conscious and satisfied.

The bed dips and I glance over to see Alec getting out of bed and holding a hand out for Darcy, who's whining about having to stand up.

"Crash here," I say without thinking, then realize I should get that kind of invite cleared first, and glance at Rafe.

He glances at me, then nods, though it's a little hesitant. "If you want to, though, if you'd rather have your own space..."

"We don't." Darcy says quickly. "I mean..."

She glances at Alec, who grins and follows her back into bed. "We don't. If you're sure, though, no pressure for you either," he directs at Rafe.

This time Rafe's grin is full and genuine. "None felt," he confirms, tugging the covers up.

And with Rafe on one side of me and Darcy on the other, Alec behind her, I've never felt quite so crowded in a king-sized bed... or quite so comfortable.

Chapter Twenty-One

THE NEXT DAY—OUR LAST full one—we briefly consider the beach but end up staying in instead. We haven't discussed it since the morning after my and Darcy's hookup, but it's our last day of... whatever this is. Because it's only a vacation fling. We can't continue it once we get home.

We shouldn't even talk about it when we get home.

Shit, have we fucked everything up?

It's not the first time I've wondered that, but every time the thought comes up it's a little more frantic. What are we doing? Are we going to regret this? Has our horniness led us so astray our friendship is unrecoverable?

I push the fears away. That's a problem for tomorrow's Bex.

Or I *try* to push them away, at least. And some activities are better at keeping them away than others.

We return the favor from yesterday and give them a show as I ride Rafe on the couch and afterwards Alec shows us what he's learned about Darcy's G-spot by fingering her to orgasm. There's another game of Twister where the goal ends up being to distract your partners enough to make them fall. I end up slipping when Darcy surprises me by licking me through my underwear.

But when Darcy and Alec talk me through deepthroating—Darcy demonstrating on Alec and Alec then going down on Rafe—I think about how I'm going to have to practice before the next time... and then remember, there *is* no next time.

I'm distracted from my worries, though, when Rafe kneels at Alec's feet.

"Can I?" Rafe asks.

Alec looks surprised at the question, looking down at Rafe with an expression that's half-awe, half-tenderness, and nods. Rafe reaches up to hook his fingers under the waistband of Alec's exercise shorts, then tugs them down, bringing his boxers with them.

There's no jealousy as I watch, just admiration for how far Rafe has come in just a few days, pleasure at how happy and excited he obviously is, anticipation at getting to watch these two insanely hot dudes get it on.

Alec is watching Rafe, though his eyes flutter shut when Rafe's tongue travels from root to tip, then swirls around the head. Rafe does this again, then again, then again until Alec's eyes are permanently closed, and when he groans, Rafe chuckles and finally takes Alec in his mouth.

He starts slow, only taking a few inches at first, then moves faster, further, and eventually he's sucking so hard his cheeks have hollowed. One hand is working as an extension of his mouth and the other is cupping Alec's balls, then slides further back. Darcy's fingers grip my thigh as Rafe's finger brushes past Alec's asshole. Oh my God is he gonna, are they gonna?

"I'm getting close—" Alec says hoarsely and Rafe jerks his hand back and hesitates for a moment. Then he pulls off Alec and stands, continuing to work Alec's cock with one hand while he buries his other hand in Alec's cropped hair and kisses him.

Alec kisses him back and it's less than a minute later when he groans, lower-half jerking as he comes against Rafe's shirt.

Foreheads pressed together, the guys breathe hard.

"Not bad for a first timer," Alec finally says and Rafe barks out a laugh then flips Alec off, who lets out a hearty chuckle.

"You can have your husband back," Rafe tells Darcy as he joins us on the couch. I slide on to his lap and give him a kiss that hopefully leaves no room for doubt that I find him as hot as ever.

But I taste Alec on him, and it brings my concerns back, full force.

Rafe just went down on someone who wasn't me.

Rafe just went down on *his best friend.*

Rafe just went down on my best friend's husband.

What the fuck are we doing?

I stand up, needing a distraction again. Needing to push the worries out of my mind. Whispering quick instructions to Rafe—who grins, nods and leaves—I turn to Darcy, who's wearing one of Alec's discarded tees and a lace thong.

"Darcy, come here," I bark, and she does. I step behind her, holding a shirt of my own up in front of her eyes, signaling my intention to blindfold her. "This okay?"

A moment's hesitation, then a nod.

"If you change your mind," I press, "what's our safe word?"

"Yellow," she says promptly. "But this is fine."

I tie the shirt around her eyes, then slowly guide her to our room. I can tell she's figured out the plan when we reach the doorway and can hear the shower running.

"Fucking finally," she says, and I laugh, giving her ass a light smack.

When she steps under the water the white shirt she's wearing turns all but transparent, clinging to every curve of her body. I see the dusky color of her areolas, the triangle of black lace between her legs, the single thread of her thong that appears above her ass cheeks and joins the other one around her waist.

I reach out for one of her breasts, rubbing a soft peak through the cloth until it turns into a hard nipple. Darcy lets out a sigh, and I nod to Alec, gesturing that the other tit is all his. His grin is wicked as he goes straight for a pinch and she starts, the soft noise escaping her sounds more like a gasp.

Her forehead wrinkles in thought as I continue gentle circles and Alec short tweaks, until finally she asks, "Wait, is that both of you?"

I laugh and she grins, but before she can continue with whatever smart-ass response she's thinking, I drop to my knees and cover her with my mouth.

"Bex." This time it's a sigh.

I motion for Rafe to give me the handheld while Alec kisses her. Then I pull away, tugging her thong off and pointing the handheld shower head at her clit.

"Fuuuuck," she groans once, and then a second time as I slide a finger inside her.

I bring her to the edge and back a half dozen times until she's begging for it. Alec pulls her shirt up over her head and brings the blindfold with it. Once she can see, she strips him of his sopping clothes and we can confirm what we'd guessed—his cock is hard and weeping.

"Already?" Rafe asks. At some point, he has stripped down as well, hand wrapped around his cock as he slowly slides it up and down his own hard length.

"Think it's your turn to undress," Darcy tells me with a grin, and I don't need to be told twice. My wet clothes join everyone else's on the bench.

Rafe slides behind me, positioning himself at my entrance and pressing a kiss to my shoulder.

"About time you joined in," I tell him, and he slides in, the lips on my skin turning to gentle teeth at my cheekiness.

He growls.

Alec's cock now has a hand wrapped around it—it's Darcy's. As they continue to kiss and I continue to stimulate her with the showerhead, Rafe's arm snakes around my waist to keep me upright and steady as he drills into me from behind.

"Bex, I'm close," Darcy warns me, and Rafe's hand sneaks between my legs, stroking my clit. My body is tight, my skin is flushed from the warm shower and exertion, and every nerve ending is tingling with awareness. It just takes a moment before I'm close too.

"Same," Rafe whispers in my ear, and Alec gives a groan that by now I recognize as his 'almost there' one.

"I'm gonna," I say, and Alec and Darcy reply in unison, "Me too". Rafe doesn't say anything but slams into me, hard, erratic. When I'm almost there, just there, *right there*, he freezes, deep inside me and his hand on my clit pushes me over the edge, and I find Darcy's G-spot and a few strokes later she moans in ecstasy, as Alec's body shudders, and somehow we're all coming together like we've practiced this, like we're used to this, like this is normal.

It feels like it should be normal.

We end up tangled with each other on the floor of the shower, warm water still pelting us. I'm half on Rafe's lap, Darcy's fingers are intertwined with mine, and I'm pretty sure Alec's cum is in my hair.

I'm satiated. Content. Exhausted. Giddy.

Terrified.

How the fuck do we come back from this?

Chapter Twenty-Two

Once we've dried off, we grab some extra pillows and everyone piles naked into Darcy and Alec's bed together, this time with the guys in the middle and Darcy and I on the outside. I wait until it sounds like everyone's asleep before I sneak out, but when I crawl between the sheets in our bedroom, Rafe is behind me.

"What's wrong, mi vida?"

I shrug, afraid that if I put my fears to words it'll become too real. I don't know how our friendship with Darcy and Alec recovers from this, how we go back to how things used to be. Even when Rafe gathers me in his arms, I'm not sure how to feel. I don't want to be jealous of Alec, but I'm very aware that Rafe's body is warm because it was tangled up with someone else's. Not mine.

He doesn't push, though. Maybe because he doesn't want to know. Maybe because he has the same doubts, and doesn't want to hear them as much as I don't want to say them.

When we wake up the next morning Darcy and Alec don't ask why we left. We're busy enough packing and stripping beds and getting ready to leave that we don't really talk much at all. It's mostly business, checking off the list left for us by the owners, but there's a tension that isn't normal.

I tell myself it's just my imagination, but when we get in the car and the silence doesn't give way to conversation and laughter, I know it's more than that. The longer we go without someone lightening the mood, the more tense it gets.

I don't know how to fix it. I tell myself we're okay, this will be fine, but can't help thinking that we broke it. We crossed lines friends shouldn't ever cross, and we didn't just put our friendships at risk. We also broke our—

No, I'm not even going to think that. Because we didn't. Our marriage vows were to love honor and cherish, not to bang only each other until the end of time. I certainly didn't picture this when I said them at our wedding, but Rafe and I being on the same page about this—even with my moments of doubt—was an act of love. I honor all parts of him, including his queerness, and that's why it was okay. We set firm boundaries that were right for us, but played within them, and there's nothing wrong with that.

Rafe and I are fine. It's our relationship with Darcy and Alec I'm not so sure about.

Rafe reinforces that we're fine when we get home, taking me by the hand and walking me to our bedroom. He peppers me with kisses as we undress each other, positioning me against the wall and dropping to his knees to go down on me. Our eyes are locked and I hold his gaze until I come, when the force of my orgasm makes me throw my head back. Then we go to our bed and he crawls on top of me, nudging my knees apart with his and slowly sliding inside me.

There's no doubt that this is about making love, about renewing our connection. Confirming that we're okay. That we can have sex with other people and still come back to each other, our relationship whole.

It's slow and luxurious, hands wandering, touching and kissing each other as our movements stay steady. And then, without discussion, we speed up—our grips a little tighter, kisses a little more sloppy, until we come, together.

The doubts I had over the past week vanish. Rafe and I are fine.

He tells me this as we lay in each other's arms, and I nod, pressing a soft kiss to his mouth.

"And Alec and Darcy?"

The thin line of his lips indicates he's not as certain about that. "I think with time we'll be fine with them too," he finally says.

I nod, and then we get out of bed to clean up and get dressed. We need to pick up the kids from my parents' house, return back to our usual schedule, where we don't fuck our best friends or have group sex in showers.

Chapter Twenty-Three

"Did you guys get into a fight?" Simon, my six-year-old, asks Rafe and me. He gestures across our backyard to the grill, where Darcy and Alec are chatting.

"Of course not, sweetie, why do you ask?" I answer.

"Usually, you're talking to Darcy and Papi is talking to Alec, but instead you're talking to each other."

This is the first we've seen Darcy and Alec for any extended period of time since they dropped us off on our driveway two weeks ago. It's only been just over fourteen days, but it feels like months.

I miss my best friend, but I'm scared I don't know how to talk to her anymore.

Rafe chooses a distraction tactic, leaning over and tickling Simon who squeals and laughs and squirms out of his grasp. Then he darts across the yard to where the rest of the kids are. Simon is the youngest of the six who are almost as close as siblings. I hope we haven't ruined things for them as well.

"You should go talk to her," Rafe says, wrapping his arms around my shoulders and folding me into his embrace. "I know you miss her."

"I do. Do you?"

"We were never as close as you two."

I pull away partially, meeting his gaze. "That's not an answer."

Rafe nods.

Pulling the rest of the way apart I weave our fingers together and tug him in the direction of the grill.

"I know I said no screens," I call to the kids. "But if you guys want to go play Mario Kart, you can."

Unsurprisingly, they all rush inside, our oldest grabbing the chips to bring with him.

"They're going to ground those into the carpet," Darcy says.

"Then he'll get some great practice vacuuming," I say, and Darcy's smile in response is still a little tight, a little awkward.

I glance at Rafe, and he raises his eyebrows at me, as if to say, *go ahead*.

I take a deep breath. "I know things are weird," I say. "But I don't want them to be. So how do we get back?"

Alec lets out a woosh of air, as if he'd been holding his breath. "Take a what happens in Vegas approach?" he offers.

"Assuming you can avoid thinking about me naked every time you see me," Darcy says teasingly, jutting her hip out and tossing her hair over her shoulder.

"And we can promise to pretend like we don't notice your nipples every time you guys eye fuck across the room," Alec adds, which makes all four of us laugh, and me blush bright red.

Rafe then growls playfully, wrapping his forearm across my breasts. "Yeah, my wife's nipples are off limits to you two," he says, then leans his head down to press a kiss where my neck meets my shoulder.

If they're going to pretend like they don't notice my nipples, I decide to also pretend like I don't notice the hunger that flashes across Alec's face as he watches Rafe.

"So we didn't ruin anything?" I confirm, and Darcy shakes her head.

"We had a vacation fling. Vacation's over, fling's over. Back to normal–well, *our* normal."

"We'll just pretend like it never happened," Rafe says, as if he didn't mutter *Alec and Darcy taught you so well, mi vida,* when I deep-throated him last week, and I nod as if I didn't moan around his cock when he said it.

"Simple enough," I agree. Because I'm sure what we remember from the trip will start to blur with time, and there'll be a point where I won't wonder if it's my imagination or if Darcy is actually looking at my mouth.

"So, do we think we're going to get our first cold front in October, or will we have to wait until November? I swear it comes later every year!" I say brightly.

Darcy just looks at me.

"What?" I ask.

She gives me an even more pointed look.

"*What?*" I press.

"We said we're not going to be awkward, so you're not allowed to talk about the weather."

"Sorry!" I say.

"NBA preseason—" Alec starts, but I interrupt him.

"No. No sports."

"The trailer for the next season of *Love is Blind* just dropped?" Darcy offers.

"That show is—" Rafe starts, but again I cut in.

"If you were going to say anything other than amazing you need to stop."

"Of course, I was going to say amazing!" he lies.

"Really?" Darcy and Alec ask in unison.

I laugh, shaking my head. "Definitely not."

Rafe snakes his arm around my waist and presses a kiss to my temple. "You gonna make me watch it?" he asks.

"Yes, so that you have something to contribute to the conversation the next time we go out," Darcy answers for me.

"I'd like that," I say. "We should put something on the calendar."

We all pull out our phones to settle on a date, and I can't deny the relief I feel that this is one step closer to what life was like before the beach trip. Because that's the direction we need to move in if we want our friendship to survive.

Still, when Darcy sends the invite it lands in my inbox as *Fourgy*, which is what she always used to label the calendar invites as, because she's Darcy and of course she did. By the time I go to my calendar she's already changed it to *Double Date*.

"Sorry," she says apologetically. "Old habits."

"It's fine," Rafe says, while I try not to remember our last night at the beach.

Because what happened on vacation that one time, will stay on vacation, that one time.

And maybe occasionally in a fantasy?

But nothing more. And thank goodness for that, because returning to life the way it was before our vacation is what's best for all four of us and our friendship. I can put the past in the past, relieved to avoid the awkwardness that would follow if we didn't.

Any lingering "what if"s will fade over time, just like the memories.

If I tell myself that enough, I'm sure I'll believe it.

Thank You, Readers!

With so many books out there (is your TBR as out of control as mine?!) it means a lot to me that you've chosen to spend your time reading this book.

Reviews help books find their readers, so I'd love if you could leave one for *Breaking Boundaries* on Amazon, Goodreads, Storygraph, and/or anywhere else you tend to buy books!

If you're curious how Bex and Rafe's first date ended, you can sign up for my newsletter at http://www.gemmablythe.com/newsletter and get that short story for free.

And for a sneak peek at whether or not the foursome is able to keep to their 'what happened on vacation stays on vacation' plan, read on for the first chapter of book 2, *Double Desire*! (Spoilers: they can't...)

Double Desire

That Bex messages me during our kids' sixth grade band concert isn't really a surprise. If you've ever been to a middle school band concert you know what I mean, and since our kids were up first, we now have another thirty minutes before the concert is over. Texting is a more socially acceptable way to pass the time than the guy a row in front of me who fell asleep on his wife's shoulder.

The surprise comes from *what* Bex sent me.

I know this, seeing as I was the maid of honor at her wedding. She was the matron of honor at mine, two years later. Being best friends since the first day of college will do that to you.

Darcy

> You doing anything fun?

Bex

> Still trying to decide. We'd toyed with the idea of just going out to some place in the hill country, get an airbnb or something.

The dots appear and disappear, like she's either taking a long time to type something, or typing and then deleting. Finally, a message comes through.

Bex

> Would you guys be interested in joining us?

When I read the question all the air leaves my body, because the immediate answer is yes, absolutely yes. But then I wonder if she's asking what I think she's asking. It's been a little over six months since the last time we went on vacation just the four of us, and we've since had an unspoken agreement never to discuss it.

Don't get me wrong, it was fun. It was a lot of fun. But it was also the kind of thing that could have totally fucked up our friendship if we'd let it get out of hand, which is why ending it when we came home was the only logical choice.

I glance over my shoulder at her, and she's staring back at me, though when our eyes meet she turns beet red and turns back to her phone.

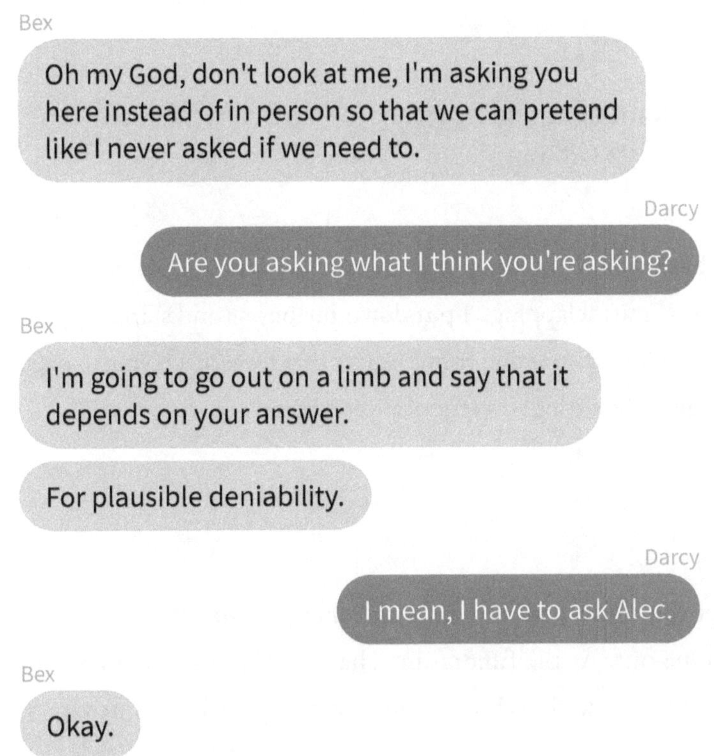

I nudge my husband, who's reading the program like it's a novel, and just as I tilt the screen towards him Bex sends another message.

I snatch the phone back, about to ask why she asked me right now if I'm not supposed to ask him right now, when my phone vibrates with another message, this one from Alec to the group text we share with Bex and her husband.

Alec

> Something you two want to share with the rest of the class?

That's when the song the seventh graders are playing ends and everyone starts clapping. I put down my phone and start clapping too, thankful for a distraction from the fact that I was just trying to negotiate an orgy while sitting in a school auditorium.

***

After the concert we mingle with other parents, waiting for the kids to come out. As the fundraising chair for the band boosters, tons of people have questions for me, but eventually we make our way to Bex and Rafael.

"You never answered the text," Alec says, wrapping his arms around my shoulders from behind. "What were you two being so secretive about during the concert?"

Bex turns bright red when our gazes meet.

"Text?" her husband asks, but when he looks at Bex they have a silent conversation, and realization dawns on his face. "Oh. Wait, you asked *here?*"

"I feel like I'm missing something," Alec says, so I wrap my hands around his forearms and give him a light squeeze.

"Their anniversary is coming up, and they were wondering if we wanted to join them on a getaway."

I keep my voice light because we're at a school, surrounded by other parents, and our kids are coming out at any moment. But I can tell by the way he goes still behind me that Alec knows exactly the meaning behind the invitation, and when I turn to look at him, he's looking at Rafael with definite heat in his gaze.

"Ye-," he starts, then freezes and looks at me to check in. It reminds me of that last trip, when we both wanted so much but also wanted to be sure the other one did too, always put our own relationship first. "I mean..."

I nod and give him the briefest of kisses because we are, after all, in the middle of our kids' school. Then I look back at Bex and Rafael. "Yeah."

Double Desire is available now!

Acknowledgements

One day in 2021, while in the query trenches with a different story, a plot bunny hopped into my brain and I jotted down one scene for my critique partners just to see what happened. Somehow, that plot bunny became a whole damn book, and there are so many people that helped me get from there to here.

First and foremost, the critique partners who read my story from the very first word: Jessica Joyce, Livy Hart, and Sarah T. Dubb–thankful doesn't begin to describe how I feel about your presence in my life. You've helped me grow in so many ways as a writer, as a reader, and as a person.

To my earliest cheerleaders, Andrea Rinaldi-Perez, Carla G, Jenny Adams, Jenny Lane, and the Bananapants. I sent you often messy chapters of my 'just for fun' project and got so many encouraging notes and emojis in response. You kept me going when I wasn't sure if there was an actual story in here.

A heartfelt thank you goes to my beta readers Lucy Birch, Mae Bennet, Scarlette Tame, and Vienna Veltman, and proofreaders, Alec Marsh, Carla G (once again!), EJ McAnoy, and Virginia Brasch. Antara Dutt, my editor, and Rae Douglas, my authenticity reader, both of who helped polish this story and make sure that I hit all the right notes.

I would also like to extend my appreciation to the online writing communities I'm in, especially Hopeful Writers and Smutfest–having a place where I can go find community among people who *get it* has been invaluable.

In addition to my online communities, I have to mention the real-life support systems who have been there for me. Carrie, Dani, Elana, and JH, the screaming hole has been a refuge through so many tricky times. Jenni, Marci, Meredith, Nate, and Sara, thank you for not dumping me from the group text even though I have an Android. And a shout-out to June and whatever real estate dieties that helped us pick a house 3 doors down from an aspiring romance author, Minecraft mom, and all around awesome lady.

If all goes as planned my parents and kids will never know I wrote this book, but I'll give them a shout out anyway, because things never go to plan.

A profound and heartfelt gratitude to my Will, who loves me on the daily, through the good and the bad.

And last but certainly not least, I am deeply grateful to anyone who has read my stories on Vella or Radish. Your comments provide the motivation I need to write the next line, the next chapter, the next book.

To everyone mentioned and to countless others, my deepest thanks and appreciation. Writing a book takes a village, and thank you for being mine.

About the Author

Gemma Blythe writes stories about love and relationships: the good, the messy, and the honest. Her love of romance blossomed in high school when unrequited crushes led her to seek happily ever afters in books and movies.

Though Gemma's stories are fiction, she's inspired by the partner she eventually found her own happily ever after with. When Gemma isn't writing, you can find her lost in the pages of a book, cooking up a storm in the kitchen, attempting to interpret her Tarot spread, and trying to convince her friends and family that she would definitely win Survivor. (She would definitely not win Survivor.)

You can find her online at www.gemmablythe.com and keep in touch with her via her newsletter at www.gemmablythe.com/newsletter